Ben Halls is a London-based
worked in pubs, off licences and s
before deciding to return to school to pursue his passion for writing. In 2014 Ben completed his Bachelor of Fine Arts in Writing, Literature and Publishing at Emerson College in Boston, MA, and completed his Master of Fine Arts at Kingston University in 2016. *The Quarry* is his debut novel.

'Halls weaves a chorus of voices that don't shy away from the ugliness of contemporary deprivation – the casual racism, the violence and addiction – but this refusal to romanticise or rose-tint is where the book's power lies. In following these flawed, multifaceted characters as their lives obliquely intersect, we're forced to reckon with a section of our society that is frequently denounced as hopeless, but is actually anything but. Halls' stories show that even in zero-hour, austerity-battered Britain, the tenderness and warmth of human connection exists. *The Quarry* is, in the end, a testament to this messy truth – how love, hate, hope and fear have always lived on the same street' Glen Brown, author of *Ironopolis*

'Halls's arresting debut tackles topics from addiction to toxic masculinity' the *i*

'Halls has a sharp observational eye, exploring both the best and worst of humanity, and how it exists side by side' Culture Fly

'Equal parts tough and tender, *The Quarry* is essential reading. Ben Halls has important insights into the challenges faced by men in post-industrial, gig-economy Britain' Alice O'Keefe

'*The Quarry* is a powerful read and you won't regret picking it up and flicking through the amazing stories. At this point of my review I'd usually list my favourite short stories from the book, but it's too hard to choose as every one of them struck a chord with me. They're all immensely powerful in their own way and each story merits a medal in its own right' *Daily Record*

'Tender, droll . . . Halls gives his flair for knuckle-chewing agony free rein' *Observer*

BEN HALLS

the quarry

DIALOGUE BOOKS

First published in Great Britain in 2020 by Dialogue Books
This paperback edition published in 2021 by Dialogue Books

10 9 8 7 6 5 4 3 2 1

A CIP catalogue record for this book is available from the British Library.

ISBN 978-0-349-70110-3

Typeset in Berling by M Rules
Printed and bound in Great Britain by Clays Ltd, Elcograf S.p.A.

Papers used by Dialogue Books are from well-managed forests and other responsible sources.

Dialogue Books
An imprint of
Little, Brown Book Group
Carmelite House
50 Victoria Embankment
London EC4Y 0DZ

An Hachette UK Company
www.hachette.co.uk

www.littlebrown.co.uk

For my mum and dad.
Without you, my dreams would still only be so.

Stories

Ham

February 8th, me dad's birthday. Every year I dig his letter out the drawer to read it, and it always puts me in a proper foul mood. Don't know why, he was a right twat sometimes, mean to me and Mum. Bit of me was glad when he up and left us, happy to get him out the house, but I was only ten and what'd I know. When he went so did the money; no more holidays or big Christmas pressies or nothing. Fridge got proper bare and the house was always freezing. He did this to us, he did. Made us fuckin' poor. Skipped the country too so the courts couldn't get him neither.

He wrote me just that once, four years back now when I was sixteen. Slipped a picture in it too; him grinning away on a lilo, drink in hand. Said he hoped I'd done me exams and wasn't quitting on school, that he'd send money if he could, but never fuckin' did. He said he was sorry too, like that'd make a fuckin' difference. Was nice, though, the massive twat that is me dad actually asking for me to forgive him. Didn't leave an address or nothing with it. Stamp on it came from Spain, down in Marbella. I never told me Mum 'bout it neither. Bit of me was glad he'd wrote to me and just me, felt special, and a bit of me didn't want to upset her. She got all odd when she weren't sat watching the telly so I thought I'd leave her be. I stuck it down the bottom of me drawer.

Decide then and there that I weren't going out with the lads tonight, gonna stay home and have a quiet one, save a bit of money. 'Cause that's the only way you get out of being poor, only chance of getting out the bloody estate; you buy your way out, and I ain't going to do that pissing me Tesco's wages up against the wall every weekend. But then I'm just foolin' meself, aren't I? You don't save enough money to get out of the Quarry by not going out. If I didn't go out, I wouldn't even do anything.

This is why I hate reading me dad's letter, gets me all wound up. I just want to know why he did it, you know? Why he took everything and left, that's all I want from him. That and some fuckin' money.

Proper fuckin' grim Saturday morning. Cold enough your breath blows smoke, even indoors. Still dark at six when I roll up to work, parking up me clapped-out Corsa next to the other beat-up motors that are at Tesco's that time of day. Sun ain't nowhere to be seen, the lazy shite. Streetlights picking up the slack.

Lock the car up and put me hands back in me pockets right proper quick. Delivery trucks are already in, sure I'll get an earful for not beating them to it. Who cares, it's six in the fucking morning. Only ones who care are the ones whose got nothing else to care about. Round the back of the store Danno's tokin' away with his eyes well shut. He's leaned up against the outside of the loading bays. I scuff a boot as I get close and he hands a jay over without saying a word. He hasn't slept yet, it's pretty blatant. Most guys smoke to try to get some kip, he smokes to come down enough to get through the shift. I take a hard drag and shut me eyes real tight, letting things spin a second or two before blowing out, then another quick puff for the head rush before handing it back.

'Y'good, mate?' I says as he puts the jay back in his lips. I pull out a Mayfair and pat around me coat till he passes me a spark.

'Safe, bruv, safe as,' he says, blowing more smoke up. The rest of the morning chain gang is behind him in the bay, looking hard at the pallets that've been cut outta their plastic shells. There's ten of us here, ten cursed bloody souls who get up and unpack smoked salmon and organic pears all morning, 'cause God for-fuckin'-bid that people could wait a bit so we could get more kip.

'Coming down The Falcon tonight?'

'Nah, bruv, not really feeling it. Might stay in, save a bit of money.' Bit of a lie, but can't say to him that reading me dad's letter got me all moody. You don't talk about that with mates.

'Didn't hear 'bout Scruff? He jacked a fruity last night, didn't he. Not even one of the casual ones down at the pub, one of the big ones up at the services. Got a repeater and all.'

'What'd he win?' Me cig gets real close to the filter, burning up more than pleasing.

'Took it all, five hundred. Matty was well pissed, he'd sunk forty into it before Scruff threw in a few quid and jacked the lot. Jammy cunt.'

'He not comin' in then?'

''Course not. He's got some serious wedge on him, he ain't getting up at six in the fuckin' morning, ya get me.'

Five hundred quid. Two weeks' take home, all things given. Lucky shit. Don't know what I wouldn't do for that kind of money.

'He spreading it around then?' I ask him, stomping me snout out.

'Yes, mate, round Matty's before, then down The Falcon. Proper good piss up.'

I give him a nod; guess we're going out. Don't even want to, but it's rare to have some money flowing. Scruff's good about it, spreads it around, so might as well have a cheap one. Might snap me out of me mood and all.

The Shift Nazi heads over, tie all awkward with his Tesco's shirt, and tap-tap-tapping away on his clipboard. He's well north of forty, been here longer than any of us, and dead proud of having that clipboard. It's his life, and what a sad fuckin' life that must be.

'Daniel, Paul,' he says in that smarmy way that tried to be cheerful and all authority at once, but just comes over sounding like a massive twat. I hate it when he calls me Paul, only me Mum calls me Paul, and only then if she were in a stress with me. To the rest of the world I was Jacky, Jacko, Jacky Boy. Kept me dad's last name, Jackson, and it basically became me given one. Me and Danno roll our eyes at each other and peel inside to get unloading.

This is how the day goes. The stuff that goes on the shelves comes in overnight. It's all wrapped up nice and tight on pallets, all counted by computers. Shift Nazi checks it all. Boys like me, Danno and Scruff then get the pleasure of cutting the plastic wrap off and putting it out on the front so peoples can get what they need. This happened six days a week – six days a week of getting up at five to get there at six in the morning. You lug boxes around till one, all for a bit over eight quid an hour. If you get done humping sooner, you get to help clean out the rotten veg and spoiled fish as a bonus. It's properly fucking shit.

We try to make a game of it. You've got to do something to keep ya mind from going wonky, they don't let you listen to music or nothing. Zero shit, they think it'd be 'unprofessional'. Seeing how many pallets you can shift in an hour's too much, too easy. Bit too obvious. You get the work done quick they cut your hours or put you on clean-up, then you'd be right fucked. What you do is see how few pallets you move each hour, but when Shift Nazi gives you shit for slacking or spies you having a crafty smoke you add a point on. You do three pallets, get caught twice, you got five points. Lowest score wins a smoke from the rest of us.

You got to do it, though. Can't not have a job, government ain't going to give you shit. All they care about are making sure the fuckin' Poles and Pakis don't get their feelings hurt. You go down the Job Centre and they'll give you fifty quid a week for a few months before cutting you off. Don't want to give you nothing. It's two years since I left school after hanging around to get me A levels, a C in Art and B in Spanish. I was the only one who stuck around to get them, the rest scarpered soon as they could. Did me no good, I'm in the same boat as the rest of them; living with our mums and getting up at five in the morning to unpack pints of milk, going round scrounging enough money to have a car to get to work with something leftover to get pissed up at the weekends. Fuckin' pathetic.

'Paul, you've got to pick it up. We've got another delivery coming in half an hour,' says the Shift Nazi.

Fuckit, that's another point. Danno smirks from across the bay and says, 'Unlucky, Jacko,' as he plays on his phone. Really could of done with those smokes. By the end of the shift some new fuckin' Pole wins 'em. Tell him to fuck off until he could ask for 'em in English and take a case of beers off his pallet as I head back to me car.

'Y'alright love, how was work?' me Mum says when I get home. She's sat in front of the telly with a full ashtray for company. Same place she's at every day since Dad went.

Actually, guess that's not fair on her. She was alright at first, looking after me and waiting for him to come home. When I grew up and the penny dropped he weren't coming back, then she got like this.

'Not bad, ta,' I say as I kick off me shoes.

'Want a spot of lunch? Think we've got some ham left.'

'No thanks, Mum. Think we're going out tonight, Scruff won a bit of money. Going to get some sleep, rest up a bit.'

'Alright, love, let me know if you want some tea later on.'

Say thanks and walk upstairs. Always the same conversation. Sad, but there ain't much else I can do. Government gives her a bit every month, least they can do, and she doesn't get worked up sat there.

Once in me room I flick the little hook lock over and throw me jacket down. I fish a pack of fags out of me work trousers then kick 'em off. Throw me work shirt off too. Sparking a cig I crawl back into bed, careful not to ash on the sheets. Turn me telly on and smoke till the fag burns down to the filter before rolling over to catch some sleep.

Standard Saturday night arrangement; me and Danno round at Matty's flat, Scruff on his way. I'd left the beers in me car but it'd been proper freezing all day so they were alright. I was supping on one watching Danno and Matty play on the console. They's calling each other all kinds of shit and I was bored, properly regretting coming out. I crush me empty can and fish out another. Matty has a nice flat. His family have money, he's just a rich kid playing poor. Wasn't at Tesco's with us, he works somewhere in central with his old man. Never says doing what, no matter how much we got on at him. End of the day we don't care that bad; he has money and doesn't live down the Quarry with his mum. His flat was full of furniture all new from Ikea or someplace like that too, no hand-me-downs.

'Where's Scruff?' I ask when they go quiet between games.

'That cheating arse,' Matty says, 'you hear what he did?'

'Yes, mate, Danno told me,' I say, but he's not listening.

'I'll tell you what he did. He fucking watched me feed coins into that fruity all night, then when I went for a smoke he stuck a few quid in and got all my money out.'

'C'mon, leave it off him. It's not like you sunk all five hundred in.'

'Doesn't matter, I put the last bit in that got it to pay out, then he comes along and reaps the benefits. It's my money.'

'You know he's good when he wins.'

Matty gives off a huff and gets back to his game. I crunch up another empty and crack the next one.

By the time I got that one down me throat, and the next one too, Scruff was ringing at the door. Matty didn't look up so I let him in. Scruff was always the little runt, and when he made his way up he was looking proper small carrying a case of beers and a few plastic bags.

'Y'alright, guys,' he says in his voice that never really broke right that we give him a mountain of shit over. Me and Danno pat him on the back to welcome him.

Matty stays round the TV, stubborn prick. 'Look who it is, the prodigal son returns,' he says. 'The lads tell me you weren't at work. Enjoying your ill-gotten gains today, were we?'

'C'mon, mate, leave off him,' I say. Don't know why Matty gets so uptight about money. Maybe he thinks that if he cares about it it'll seem like he has less. Don't know what it is with people wanting to look like they got less than they do.

'I bought this for everyone,' Scruff says, opening up the case of beers, 'y'know how it is when you've got some cash.'

Scruff went into his plastic bags and brought out a half-bottle of something for everyone. Pack of cigs each too, proper ones and all; not any shit brand or ones out the back of a truck.

'C'mon, Matty,' Danno says, unscrewing the cap on his bottle, 'get off it and let's have a night.'

Matty walks over and gives Scruff a shove that was a little too hard to be playful but fuckit he's here. The rest of us unscrew our caps and take big, long gulps. It burns like fuck but we don't care, it's why you unpack pallets at six in the morning.

The Falcon is proper full. All the dregs drink there; Quarry locals looking for a cheap one, the school kids looking for anyone who'll serve them, the old boys who've been going there since 19-fuckin'-forever. Dad used to drink down here before he got out and left, or so me Mum says. Whenever I'm down here I wonder if some of the old boys at the bar knew him, if he ever bought them a drink or something. I'd ask them if it weren't so sad, going up to the old drunks and asking if any of them knew me dad 'cause I didn't.

It ain't even ten and we's all smashed up. I mean properly twatted. We'd finished the bottles in the flat, along with the beers, and were three or four deep down the The Falcon already. You get a routine going: drink a beer, have a piss, outside to smoke a cig, repeat. World's going a little bit blurry, and having a slash me aim's all akimbo. When I bust outside for a smoke the snout goes down in what's like one big breath, so I take another straight away and light it with the cherry from the last.

I've lost track of the rest of the lads till I see them trying it on with a couple of girls. They were pretty fit, but there was only two of them. Matty and Danno look like they's the ones making moves, and Scruff lookin' proper sorry for himself. Made me right angry; typical childish bullshit Matt'd pull, making Scruff feel like shit just for getting a break. Danno don't know better than to go along with it all. And fuck Scruff too, letting them beat up on him like that. Really regretting coming out now, I might have been all miserable sitting at home with me mum but least I wouldn't need to worry 'bout this.

I stumble on the fuckin' step as I head back inside and the Gorilla Bouncer catches me eye. I give him a little smile and nod; yeah, yeah, I tripped, but I'm fine, ya cunt. It's Saturday night at a pub, we gonna be sat around with cuppas? No need to toss me, least not yet.

I get behind the scrum at the bar and feel around me pocket for a note. Can't find any paper, but there's a fuckload of coins so I pull out some shrapnel and start sifting through. Got me head down when this elbow comes up and hits me hand, sending the coins scattering. It belonged to some pikey shite with more gel on his head than hair.

'Watch it,' I say, throwing in a snarl.

'Fuck off,' he says, giving me a shove as he turns his Ugly Head back to the bar. Twat. The coins are lost under the swarm of feet, at least an-hour-and-a-bit's pay – over an hour of slinging corned beef – just gone. With me lighter in me fist I punch the twat round the back of his head.

He stumbles forward and someone drops their drink. I get one more solid shot in at his kidneys before I feel a hand on me shoulder. I spin round quick with me arm cocked but see the Gorilla Bouncer on me and think better of it. I let him pull me out the scrum before remembering me coins. I try to say that I need to go back and get 'em, that I know I'm done but just want me money, but what comes out is slurred shite and he ain't having none of it.

Out on the street on me fuckin' arse and Gorilla's saying something at me, but I ain't listening. Standing stable as I can I wander off down the side where the smokers are. The lads are still there, still chatting with the girls and making Scruff feel like proper shit. I manage to snag Matty's attention, who says something to the girls and gets as close to me as the barrier lets.

'Bruv, got kicked,' I manage to get out. I know I got a slur on, so fuck knows what I sound like to other people, 'some wanker was being a right twat. You coming?'

'What? Leaving? Fuck that. I think we're gonna stay here with the girls for a bit. We'll let you know if we head to the flat, though.'

Matty turns himself round and goes back to the rest of the lads, just like that. Well, fuck him too, then. Shouldn't have fuckin' bothered with tonight. It's always the same shit.

I fish around in me pockets for a lighter but the Gorilla Bouncer has followed me round the corner and is telling me to get away. I ask him to kindly fuck off and say that I'm going, and make me way to the Paki shop to get a lighter and something for the way home. It gets easier to walk after I lean against the side of Boot's to chuck in the road. Ain't nothing in it but liquid and it steams up. Fuckin' disgusting, but the world ain't all sideways no more. I cut through a car park behind a posh office building and take a piss against some twat's BMW.

Make it to the Paki shop. It's empty 'cept for the lone guy behind the counter. He shoots me a proper evil eye. Fuck him and his stupid thin beard. Probably gave a half of vodka to some fifteen-year-old for a blowie. Got that telltale coke nail and all. At the shitty fridge and looking for a drink, I'm rooting around in me pocket trying to figure out what I got enough for when I hear it.

'That's the fuckin' cunt!'

It's the Ugly Head from the bar who'd elbowed an hour and a half of unwrapping frozen shepherd's pies out of me hand. He's got red on his shirt, so I must have opened him up. Got a mate with him too, a big mean-lookin' fucker with his head shaved. 'Course I'm by me jack, 'cause me mates would rather chat up girls. Before I know it one comes down each aisle and I'm trapped by the Ginsters pies. The Paki behind the counter has looked up from his phone and is yelling something at us, and I make a charge at Ugly Head 'cause I'd much rather have another pop at him than his Big Mate. I drop me shoulder and send him sprawling into a rack of crisps. He grabs at me as we collide, but I'm fuckin' buzzed now and it don't hurt. He tries to land a few too but lets go and topples over. Big Mate looks to be lining me up for a punch, but he's slow and I grab at the door proper quick to get me back onto the street.

I jog to get a little distance between me and the Paki shop before looking back. Ugly Head's up again and on the street with his Big Mate. He's shouting, and I tell him to fuck off over and over till Big Mate passes him something. He flicks it open and flashes the blade at me before yelling some more and making a run at me. Quick as I fuckin' can I turn on my heels and take off.

For a bit I listen out behind me for his shouting and screaming before just concentrating on me running. I ain't ever been quick, but I ain't ever run for me life before either. It's not like regular running. This is fuckin' primal; I slip, he'll fuckin' knife me. It's only when I'm well away from town, deep back in the Quarry, that I take a real quick look behind me. Ugly Head and Big Mate are nowhere to be seen. He's probably slipped or given up, maybe the police had got him.

There's no stopping, though, and I jog back to me house. Me keys are out quick as I can and when I get inside I rest me head against the door. The coldness of it is fuckin' bliss. Slowed down I can feel me heart thump in me chest, and me knees are a little weak. Feel sick again. Breathing is all I can do, eyes closed and trying to get some fuckin' air in me.

'That you, love?' me mum says from the living room. Fucksake, I say to meself, now I've got to go through this pantomime.

'Yeah,' I says back between breaths, not opening me eyes.

'You're back early.'

'Bit tired from work, is all.'

'You want something to eat? I think there's some ham.'

'No thanks, Mum.'

I push meself away from the door and poke me head into the living room. Clock says it's nearly one in the morning.

'You're out of breath, love. Didn't jump another taxi, did you?'

'Yeah,' I says to her, 'I didn't realise I was out of money till I got back.'

'You shouldn't do that. You heard what the policeman said last time, if you did it again he'd take you in for it.'

'I know, won't do it again, Mum.'

'You sure you don't want something to eat, love?'

Don't think I could eat a thing ever again. We say our goodnights and I head up to me bed. Me clothes get thrown in the corner, and when I go for a piss before sleeping I chuck again. The telly's turned on quiet for the noise and light and I try to sleep, but it ain't coming. Doesn't come till long after the sun's back up, and I miss me Sunday lunch sleepin' late. I don't care, I just lay there. Mind made up, I'm staying here till work. At one point I go to have a fag, but don't have a light.

Monday morning can piss clean off. It don't snow no more, but it can frost up something shite. Me windscreen is frozen solid. Takes me ages to scrape it clear, so I pull into Tesco's late. Start a cigarette with the car's lighter and get half of it in me by the time I get over to the bay. The Shift Nazi starts saying something about me timekeeping, but frankly I couldn't give less of a shit and tell him so. He looks a bit pale at that. There's a pallet waiting for me so I get me head down. Danno and Scruff are there and might have tried to give me a nod, but I wasn't looking.

Pallet was done right proper quick, next one too. Shift Nazi makes a crack 'bout not working like this all the time and lets me go get a cuppa. I pour meself one and head to the car park for a smoke. It's nearly ten and the sun was only now starting to show its face, like it's ashamed of the shithole it oversaw. I pat around in me pockets for me missing spark, swearing to meself a bit. Don't want to think of why it weren't there, don't want to think of what happened. Just want to get work done and then back to bed. I only notice Danno's walked over when he holds out a light.

'Where'd you end up this weekend, bruv? Gave you a bell but never heard from you.'

'Just stuff, mate,' I says back. Don't want to get into it.

'You missed a fuckin' ball. We met these girls down The Falcon, and let me tell you; fuckin' filth. Absolute fuckin' filth. Me and Matty holed up in his flat the rest of it, had a sick time.'

'Sorry, mate. Couldn't make it.'

'You meet a girl or something? Keeping it secret?'

'Nah, bruv.'

'Sure you are. Worried Matty's going to get jealous and try and bang her, that it?'

'Just drop it, will ya?'

'Alright, what's up your arse today?'

'Look at us, it's just fuckin' pathetic,' I say and walk back inside.

I want to say more. I want to tell him how fuckin' stupid it is; these are our lives here, happening right now. This is us, and what do we do with them? We get high and we get drunk and we live with our mums, paying for it all by unpacking sliced fuckin' ham. You wouldn't want to know what I did with my weekend, Danno, ya waste. Most of all you wouldn't care. I stayed in school, I did, all the way up to eighteen. I got me A levels and knew people who'd gone off to uni and who'd have proper jobs with desks and suits and everything. People who'd moved out of the Quarry, got into London proper. I fuckin' knew what else was out there, and still I was stuck here with you.

Me weekend was getting pissed off at some stranger for knocking a few coins out of me hand, and nearly getting stabbed for it. Didn't even want to fuckin' be there, but it's all there is to do. And you want to know the worst of it? If I hadn't chucked down the side of Boot's then Ugly Head's knife would've been sticking out of me guts. Would have been too pissed to run otherwise, easy pickings for him. No, mate, I wasn't shacked up with some girl or nothing. I was running around leading this fuckin' pathetic life that we go out and lead and nearly getting killed for it. So yeah, I'm fuckin' done. I'm done with you and Scruff and most of all that arrogant twat Matty.

But I don't say that to him. Don't even know how I would. You don't talk about this shit, you're just supposed to get on with it; keep yer head down and stay tough. Instead of talking I stamp on me snout and push me hands back into me pockets. Shift Nazi says something to me about needing to get back, but I shoot him a look that says it ain't happening. He lets me walk right on past him and into the back locker room that all us grunts use. It's empty and I take advantage, stalking about all riled up. Nobody's gonna bother me in here.

What the fuck am I even doing, stacking shelves at fuckin' Tesco's? Twenty years I've been alive, twenty years to do something, and what? I done nothing. I finished school, and what for? Did what me dad wanted, stayed all the way up till eighteen like he said in his letter, and why? To give me the necessary fuckin' life skills to unpack chutney.

I kick a bench and kick a wall too, and then kick Shift Nazi's office door. It opens; the dumb fuck never locked it. I storm in, wanting to do something against the twat who lets me brain rot while he checks things off his fuckin' list.

It's a tiny room, desk and computer in a cupboard. I sit in his chair and glare at the door, wishing he'd come in and sack me, give me an excuse to go do something else. But he ain't coming, he's scared of me, scared of all of us, knows we only do what he tells us 'cause we need the jobs. I pull at the drawers and then fuckin' bingo: dull twat left a burlap cash bag sitting there.

Anger drops right down, thinking much more clear now. Shift Nazi handles the floats for when the overnight cashiers check out. He counts it out and seals it all up before we all show up. It's not even his job; we all knew some lazy night manager throws him a bit of cash to do it so they could get home earlier. And here was the proof, a bag all counted up and ready to go off to the bank.

I stuff it into me fleece. This store owed me something, anything, and I was gonna take it. If this place gets me so riled up I'll smack a guy for making me drop a few quid, then this is me compensation. I get out of his office right proper quick, not gonna get caught now. Shift Nazi's there in the loading bay, asking me if I'm ready to get back to work. Nah, mate, I tell him, not today. Not feeling great. Something up with me gut, going to head home. I put me hand over me middle, half to show him where it was s'posed to be hurting and half to hold the bag, and then I just go.

I drive home real careful like. Don't want nothing getting in the way of me and me bag, no plod taking an interest. When I get home and park up I don't bother with the chit-chat with me mum asking me if I want some ham. It's straight up to me room and emptying the cash sack out onto me bed. It's more money than I've ever fuckin' seen; bag of tens, bag of fives, a ton of baggies of pound coins and some random notes floating about. All laid out proper it was about two grand. Two fuckin' grand. Near enough two months' pay, all right there at once.

Know I have to do something with it, had to go somewhere, just get up and go. I weren't going to squirrel it away or pay for a few big nights out, no fuckin' way. I'm out the Quarry with this. I dig me duffle bag out and start throwing some of me clothes into it. First of all I started putting me jeans in there, but then thought fuck that, I was going somewhere hot, so took 'em out and threw in some shorts. Threw the bags of cash in there too, but not before I'd emptied the five hundred quids' worth of tens into me wallet. It's good having that much just sitting there, it's hefty and I could feel it on me arse when I sat down.

Getting me passport out of the drawer I stop right dead. Sitting back there with it is me dad's letter. I look at the envelope, sent from happy Spain, and that picture of him on a lilo. He looked happy. I think that was what I hated the absolute fuckin' most about it; he looked happy when we were fuckin' miserable. Then and there I know where I'm taking me money, what I'm doing with it. Slipping the letter in me passport and zipping me bag up I head back down the stairs. At the door I hear me mum say something or other.

'What you say, Mum?' I say back to her. She's still sat in the armchair, ashtray in lap.

'I said you going out again, love?'

'Yeah, Mum, think I am. Might have a few shifts off, so might go round Matty's for a bit. Play some games, watch some films, that kind of thing. Not too sure when I'll be back.'

'It's nice they gave you a bit of time off. Go have fun, Matthew's a nice boy.'

I get to the door before shouting back one last time. 'Mum?'

'Yes, love?'

'You—' and then I stop. I want to say to her that I love her, that I'll be back soon, that maybe things'll be different when I am, but I'm not sure how much of any of that's true. I'm not even thinkin' 'bout coming back, I'm just thinkin' 'bout leaving. I know I got to do something, though, so I open up me wallet and put some of the wedge that's in there in the pocket of her coat. Better than me old man ever did, least I was leaving something. She shouts out again and I mumble something to her before bolting to me car so that I can't bottle it.

Only been to Heathrow once, on me holidays when Dad were still about. Still, knew how to get there alright – A40, M40, M25, half-hour max. As I'm getting along I've the thought 'bout what'll I do when the Shift Nazi figures out the cash bag's gone. Work lets off in a bit over an hour, he could well spy it then. Is there even a camera in there? Fuck, I don't know. He probably won't check it till he clocks back in tonight, and by then I'll be away and on the fuckin' hunt. They don't find the fuckin' proper criminals down in the south of Spain, doubt they'll put up much of a search for a few grand from Tesco's. By the time they clock it's me I'll have a drink with a stupid umbrella in it in me hand and some foreign girl on me cock. I'll have tracked me dad down too, showing his photo to anyone and their donkey till I find the twat. It won't matter, none of what I've done here will.

I'll walk the beach all day when I get there, asking every Spanish cunt I can find if they know him. Put that Spanish A level that me dad was bloody adamant I hung around for and got to some good use. Won't take much searching to track me dad down anyway, he'll be a local celeb, guarantee it. First thing I'm doing is asking how he can be so happy while we're so fuckin' miserable. There he is in that photo, grinning in a pool, while I'm working a shit job and me mum just watches telly all day. He did this to us, and I want to know why. I need me some compensation from him too, for leaving his kid to go hungry and lonely and shiver in bed in the winter. He'll stutter and try to charm and say he's sorry but it won't matter. I got ten years of angry in me, and I'll put it to use on him. Between every hit I'll make sure he knows just why it's happening to him. This is for Mum, I'll say, and this is from me, and this is for leaving, and this is for being happy when we ain't, and worst of all this is for making me believe that there is something else out there. This is for making me stay in school and telling me it'll help, when really it is all for shit and I'll end up in the same place as me idiot mates anyway. This is for leaving me in the fucking Quarry.

But he might not even know how bad off we are. Yeah, that's it, he doesn't have a clue. Me dad wouldn't leave us that bad off if he knew. He's got money in Spain. I can see him now, owning a little bar down there on the beach front. Nothing too touristy but offering the expats somewhere familiar to eat sausage in a basket and watch *EastEnders*. Bingo on a Thursday night. Watch the footie, bet on the horses. He always was a people person. Wish he could have been a family one instead, but ya get what ya get.

I'll walk in and spot him but he won't notice. I'll order me a beer and have a few drinks, and he'll keep looking my way knowing he knows me but not being able to place it. When I'm good and ready I'll go up to him and just say, 'Y'alright, Dad,' and he'll clock it then and there. He'll fuckin' break down, here was his boy come all the way to Spain to find him. He'll fuckin' beg me – beg me! – for forgiveness, just like he did in his letter. I can see it all right now. He'll get a bottle a something from behind his bar and we'll sit out by the beach and drink it all the way down till the stars are out blurred together in the sky and we're all square. The two grand I've got will be piss in the sea 'cause he'll give me twenty plus change to make up for the decade he's been gone. He'll know I'm smart, be proud I stayed in school, give me a job and that'll be me set. Won't have to think about me shithead mates no more, won't have no worries, 'cause I'll have me dad back.

I'll call me mum, tell her I'm sorry for leaving too but it's okay, I found Dad. Tell her he's sorry, that there's money coming in now. That it'll all work out, that it'll all be okay now. Yeah, that's how it'll be. She can get out the Quarry, move somewhere nice down by the seaside. Maybe she'll even get to fly out and we can have a Christmas together, sitting down by the beach eating a turkey. It'll be warm and we can give each other all the presents we never did before and it'll all be fuckin' bliss.

Getting closer to Heathrow I put me foot through the floor and close right up to some granny going slow in the outside lane. Give her a little flash of the lights and she gets the message. Beep beep, Gran, can't wait around for you all day, I've got me somewhere to be.

Little Ones

I knew the lad was going to kick off. You can see it in them; all that anger inside, it's toxic. Throw some drink into it and everything bubbles over. People say that they never see it coming, the swing of the fist that kicks it all off, but I can tell. They go through this change, washes over them, and you can see that they've decided to lamp someone and not give a shit. Usually I get to them before that, try and keep them safe. Not this time.

At the bar, banging into one another, clamouring to get another cheap one down their necks. The Falcon is always like that on a Friday. I saw them knock, saw the young lad – couldn't be more than twenty – go for it. He got one in, but I grabbed him after that. Had his lighter in his hand too, all vicious like. Something must have made him real angry inside.

I throw him out, but he hangs around the side where his mates are smoking and I have to chase him off. He tries to say something to me, but he's so far gone it's just a dribbling babble that falls out of his mouth. Head back round the front and offer the guy he lit up some help. Back of his head is opened up pretty bad, dripping jam onto his shirt. Tell him we'll get an ambulance, call the police, that kind of stuff. He doesn't want any of it, just grabs his mate and heads out. Asks me which direction the kid I threw out went, had to tell him I didn't know. Knew what they were going to do, didn't want it to happen and wasn't going to help it out, but once they leave there's not much I can do. Give the local PCSO a bell, tell her to look out for a young guy with blood on his shirt on a mission. She tells me they have three in the back of the van already, and it isn't even midnight.

I get back to the door and pull the collar of my coat up, nod for one of the younger guys to go inside and watch the floor for a bit. My breath's steaming up in front of me, but I need the air. It's too loud inside and all the old boys have gone home, leaving only the kids to drink up whatever money they've got.

'Getting too much for you in there, gramps?' asks Prescott, the other doorman out in the cold. He's a good kid, not much older than the lads inside but on the right path; finished uni, sweet girlfriend, boxes a fair bit to keep himself clean. Still coaches the kids a bit too.

'Just need to come up for a bit of air,' I say, 'you got the note from your mum letting you stay out this late?'

'Funny. Funny man you are there, Joseph. Am going to have to knock these late nights on the head soon, though.'

'Getting some stick from the missus?'

'Not really that, nah,' he says, showing off his youth by grinning as he kicks his feet at the pavement. I let him stew, know he'll speak up eventually if he wants to. Don't want to get into it if he doesn't.

'It's early days yet,' he says right on cue, 'and I'm not

supposed to be telling people and stuff, but it looks like we've got a little one on the way.'

He looks up at me, teeth ear to ear, that look in his eye that says he's happy, real happy, and the world don't have him by the throat at the minute.

'As I said,' he carries on, 'early days yet. Supposed to wait three months and all that. You know, just in case. But yeah, exciting stuff. Thinking I should start looking for something a little more orthodox, be home for the night feeds, you know.'

'I'm happy for you,' I say to him, meaning every word. He nods, looking off at the streetlights.

Always knew this job wouldn't stick with him. It's good money, handy casual work that kind of lad – a big guy, one that the kids with three too many in them wouldn't mess around with, except with nothing mean in him, never looking for hassle to kick off – but he's not a lifer like me.

'You got any little ones?' Prescott asks me straight out of nowhere. The question lands funny; the lads on the door turn up, do their job, go home. You're mates, watch each other's backs and all that, some of them talk about families if they have them, and want to, but most stick to themselves. You don't make proper friends here, don't have time. Been doing work like this for nearly twenty years now, never worked with one bloke longer than two years.

'Coming on all sentimental already?' I say to him. Not eager to talk, but I like the kid. His dad weren't around, don't really know who else he's got that bit older to talk to. Don't want to shut him down straight off.

'Just excited, mate, you know? I mean, all my mates who've got little ones, it's all typical Quarry shit. Casual, don't wear nothing, then nine months later there it is. Sure they love their kids, most of them anyway, but it's not like this. Don't know anyone who actually wanted their kid before it turned up, like we do. Not even me own mum.'

He's looking at me, real confused, with these big white doe eyes standing out against his dark skin that I knew the barmaids melted for. Can tell he doesn't really know how to handle it. I don't want to talk, don't do this kind of thing at work, but it's sad. Here's this kid, lot going for him, bright future and all that, and doesn't even know how to look forward.

I think about giving him the what's-what for when you get a kid of your own, but behind me I hear the telltale blast of music, folding from soft to loud and back again as someone walks out the front into the street. I look behind me, feel the old instinct kick in as I prepare for a bit of trouble, but it's just a girl walking out, red eyes with black-laced tears, followed out by a lad. Neither of them are that old. She was a beauty, though; light brown hair, little black dress, clearly wasn't local. Bit more Prada than Primark about her. Probably one of the girls whose families got out when they were younger, or never lived round here but knew a few from school. Guy following was local; never gave us any trouble at the door, and hid it well, but he was.

I look over at Prescott as the two walk out into the street. It's the dead time of night. Nobody else is going to be coming in, but the crowd won't head to the local club for another hour or so; the kids would rather sup on our cheap drinks than the club's overpriced stuff. You always get a few heading out front like this; couple too many bevvies and a bit too much emotion, wanting a bit of quiet to have it out. Not supposed to, but I'll give them the space if they need it.

'C'mon, Sammi, I didn't mean it like that, did I?' says the lad while the girl pulls a long slim cigarette out of her handbag and lights it. Prescott looks at me, asking if we should be moving them round the side to where the smokers are supposed to go, but I give him a shake of the head to tell him to leave it. They're not hurting anyone right now, and look like they need the room to talk.

''Course you did, everyone does,' she says, blowing smoke as she talks. Think I was wrong about her; she does sound local after all. Not often I'm wrong about that.

'I didn't, honest. Thought you'd be used to being recognised, anyway.'

'Yeah, I am, and it's one thing when people come up to us telling me they're a fan and stuff. It's something else when they bang on about it like you've been.'

Both kids are drunk, far gone enough to not care about what they say but still in control. She lights another butt with the cherry from her first one, he looks at his shoes not knowing what to do.

'You know I didn't mean it like that. Nothing like that. Just meant that I recognised you, your job, is all,' he says again.

'Was that the whole reason you spent the night chatting to us, yeah?'

'What, no,' he says, whipping his head up from his laces, little bit hurt, little bit panicked, 'I didn't clock it till just before I said it. Didn't know if I should even say anything, wish I didn't now, causing all this.'

'What? So you think I am ashamed?'

'Didn't mean it that way, I don't know. It's not like I'm asking for a say, am I? I was just asking for your number and to get a few drinks. Thought the other stuff was banter, I'm sorry.'

'Fuck off you were, the way you were going on about it after I told – I told you – to stop,' she says, getting right teary red and a bit loud. She holds a finger to her eye to stop a tear trashing her eye make-up and the guy looks up. I catch his eye, give him the look to tell him that keeping it down would be the better option. He gives the slightest of nods, and I can tell he's trying to figure out how to tell her to take it down without making the whole thing worse.

'Everyone thinks the same,' she says, calmer now by her own mind, firmly talking over whatever he was trying to say, 'at least the ones who don't know me, don't know the job, think it. She cams, she's got her premium snap, she sells clips and makes vids, so she'll be an easy fuck. Do it like a proper pro too – after all, she basically is one – all filthy like. I can see it in them.'

'I didn't think that, though, not really, did I, just trying to be a bit cheeky,' he says back quickly, finally getting a word in. 'Didn't even clock it till an hour or two of chatting anyway. Yeah, I think you're pretty, think you're fucking gorgeous, might have been why I came over at the start, but I wasn't thinking about that other stuff. Wasn't talking to you 'cause I thought you were, you know, something bad, 'cause of what you do and all.'

'I love what I do,' Sammi says back to him, real firm like, 'and not just because of the money. And not just because it makes me feel good, either. It's hard, and I love that. I've got to be my own camerawoman, own director, own editor. Do me own marketing, own accounts and taxes and the like. Look for outfits, keep up to date with what's hot, do all that make-up. Get myself to the gym, eat right, to look like this at all. It's hard, and it fucks me off when people just think the one thing.'

She stops, lighting a third snout when she realises she's just puffing on a filter with the one she's got. Goes a bit quiet, and I can see her looking off over the lad's shoulder, back down the street leading to the estate.

'I know, I know, look, listen, yeah? Why don't we go for a walk, go somewhere and talk. Or go back in, it's fucking freezing. I weren't coming up to you because of your job, alright? None of my business, think it's kind of cool, really.'

'What, cool like I've got to be a great fuck because for a hundred quid I'll say your name while I touch myself down a camera at you?'

'Fuckin' hell, no, nothing like that—'

'It's what you said inside.'

'And I was wrong, wasn't I! Fuck, it's got nothing to do with that, not really. It's different. It's interesting. You've made something. I get it, I was wrong, alright? You don't like it when blokes think things because of your job, I get it. But we were sat in there for hours chatting, and it was great. Why don't we go back in and carry on with that, yeah?'

'So, then what? You'd be okay with me doing what I do? We go for a drink now, then you sit at home tomorrow night while I'm on cam?'

'Christ, I'm not asking to marry you, am I? I've enjoyed chatting and drinking with youse, and I want to do it more.'

I could see her look at him, see the little wheels turning in her head. It's hard, I see it in a lot of the pretty ones. Bloke'll never come up to her 'cause of what they hear her talking about, just what's in her dress. I hope she lets him in, though. He looks like a good kid, and she seems to have her head screwed on. Seen a lot of worse matches go an awful lot further.

She nods, stepping on her cigarette and she leads him back in with the uneasy truce in place. Don't know what'll happen to them. Kid gives me a nod as he goes by, little way of saying thanks for the space. I look stern, don't want to but can't have them taking their liberties. I track the pair inside, hear them get sealed in with the rest of the noise. Look back up and Prescott's got a grin.

'That's a good one, that is,' he says, bit of energy in him from the show, 'don't see that every day. She's got to be too pretty for that, though.'

'For what? Her job?'

'One of those girls on the internet, man. I mean they're fit, yeah, used to watch them before I met Janine, you know? Never paid one, of course, but if they looked like her . . . she's something.'

'I don't watch that kind of thing,' I say, trying to get back on with keeping an eye out for a spot of trouble. Don't like looking at the girls who come in that way. I know a lot of the younger guys do, and you'd be shocked if you heard what some of the real young girls offer the lads on the door to get in, but it's never interested me.

'I tell you, mate, if my little one comes out a girl, and winds up doing that shit, I'd put a stop to it straight off,' Prescott says, blowing into his hands as the night starts to bite big chunks out of us.

'You don't know what you're talking about,' I say to him, 'cause he doesn't. He's stuck in that theory zone, where it's easy to sit and chat in absolutes – can do this, can't do this, will do this, mustn't do this. Life, real life, isn't like that.

'I'm telling you, man,' he says, smiling away, 'I'm not raising no girl like that.'

'Like what?'

'The kind of girl who sells her nudes while sad fucks have a wank at her Snapchat. Not my little girl, not if I have one.'

'What, so it was fine for you to watch it, or if you get a kid boy for him to?' I ask him, words tripping out my mouth before I can catch them.

'It's different, though, isn't it,' he says, that squirm in his step that gives away he hasn't thought about it before, 'got to keep your little one honest. Lot of shit caught up in that. Wouldn't let her in a place like this one neither, know what goes on.'

'Look, you ask me if I've got a little one. Yeah, wife and I had one. Jenny, her name was. Sweet little girl.'

'No shit, mate? You never mention it.'

'It's work, not a bloody social club, is it? This is just me and you talking now, 'cause I think you need it, alright, mate?' I say to him, trying to find the balance in my head of telling him what he needs to hear and keeping my life just to me. He nods, eyes all narrow with interest. I take a breath to keep going, knowing he'll keep it quiet.

'Anyway,' I say, 'I had her. Don't see her that much any more. At least, not like I'd like to, you know? She's in my life a lot, I'm not really with her. She's off with her mum these days.'

'They not round here any more?'

'Nah, they're a long way off. Wish they weren't, but there isn't much you can do.'

'Could find a gig like this near them, I'm sure. You're good at it.'

'Won't lie, sometimes I think about it, calling it a day down here and moving up there with them, but it's all easier said than done. Still, you figure it out when you get one of your own. Don't matter what they do, it boils down to simpler things than that. Are they safe? They happy? Got money? Not lonely? Not cold, not hungry? That kind of thing. Don't care how they wind up a good person, just want them to be one.'

'No shit. How old is she?'

'She'd be coming up nineteen now.'

'Christ, didn't even know you were married, let alone a grown-up kid. Got any pictures and stuff?'

'Not for the likes of you,' I say, stiffening back up, rubbing me hands together. I gave him his lesson, he don't need to hear any more. Wasn't the time or place, and I'm not one for teaching.

'Alright mate, alright,' Prescott says.

He looks like he wants to keep going, keep digging, but the doors open up again behind us, except this time it's a crowd of them heading out. I check my watch and it's about midnight. We keep the drinks going for another half-hour, the club lets them in for another hour, so it's crossover time. Most of them will head that way and be the club's problem, though a few'll stay for us to sweep up. They'll be the ones worse for wear who need the most help.

Talking time's over, and the night wraps up with relentless requests for the kids to move on quietly, not hang around, leave their drinks inside if they weren't finishing them, all that usual stuff. Same lot every week, think they'd know by now. I spy Sammi and the guy from earlier, turning away from the masses and heading their own way. She has her heels off, holding them over her shoulder, and hurries alongside him. I wish them the best in my head while I encourage two lads who'd had too much to not bother with the fight brewing between them and go home. They advise me where I could fuck off to, and just how many times I could, before heading their own ways.

Isn't any more trouble for the night. The PCSO comes by, tells me about a fight round at the corner shop, probably to do with who we threw out, that they might need the tape footage from us. Tell her no problem. While she's here she handles giving a girl who we found passed out in the toilet a lift to the hospital. These things are why I tell them to bring in more women to help us out, who can go into the ladies real easy and check for trouble, but they never do. Who knows what'd happen to her in there, and it's not right hoping that a barmaid notices something going on when she goes in to use them.

Prescott and the rest of the boys on the door ask me to stay for a pint once the pub was locked down and clean, but I tell them not tonight. Done enough talking. They'll sit there, give each other some grief, chat football with the barman and maybe hit on some of the girls who work there. I'm not feeling like that tonight, instead I head to the car and listen to the radio while the air warms up to get the mist off the windscreen. Takes an age, so I settle back and listen to the DJ give lorry drivers the traffic updates and send messages to people on the road that they're being thought of. The two o'clock news comes and goes.

It's an easy drive home at this time of night, only fifteen minutes, but I don't go for it. Don't really feel like banging around the house. Not really tired either; your world gets all wonky working into the night like this, clock off around two, get home and have a bit of tea, you don't get to bed until most are back off to work. Summer's the worst, birds singing you to sleep in the morning.

I turn right out the car park in my clapped-out Fiesta – could replace it, but why bother? It runs fine, don't need anything bigger or faster – and drive away from The Falcon, opposite direction to home. I like driving at night, something peaceful about it. See the town all lit up, wonder where the other cars on the road are off to. Like the mindlessness too; something mechanical about it, you've got to pay attention just enough to stop the little voice that runs through your head.

Flick the radio off of the DJ and his messages, instead

put it on one of the local talk ones. It's alright at night: a few lost souls, few lonely people, lot of nutters. Good for a chuckle, good for a thought. I've pulled over sometimes and called in. Not like one of the regulars – some of them will be on at the same time every night – but sometimes, if the mood takes me after work, I will.

I drive into London. It's nice coming in from the west; see the roads come together and rise up into one over Hammersmith, get a look at the tall towers around Canary Wharf lit up in the background, beacons as you drive towards them. I go through Kensington on the way there, then back along the Thames towards Big Ben and onwards into the West End. It's beautiful; old buildings lit up in swathes of dark blues and warming yellows, the colours bouncing off the river. Think my favourite bits are the boats. They look the best all lit up, swaying with the wake of the river. Lights on them are functional mainly, stop any traffic down the river overnight banging into them, but that doesn't stop it being something to look at. You get a few that are lived in year-round, and you can see the fairy lights twisted around the lines. Could be anywhere looking at them. Everything is gold and green along the river.

Took Jenny and her mum to Portsmouth once to look at the boats. Nice day out in the summer and all that. She was just a little thing then, slept all the way down, and loved it when we were there. Did a lot down there, bit of shopping and played at the old-fashioned arcade they got, but it was the boats she loved best. Bought her a little fishing boat model – nice one too, not a plastic thing you're supposed to take in the bath but a wooden one that's meant to be on a shelf, but she insisted on taking it in there anyway – that was so pretty. Green hull, white cabin, gold bits on the tops of the masts. Just beautiful. Never hard to get her to take a bath after that. Her mum thought it was a waste, taking a nice model like that to get ruined in the water, but it made her smile and got her off to bed easy.

In the West End there are still people, mainly stumbling home or heading to the casinos to bridge the gap between the last and first trains. Makes me smile seeing that there's life in the city, even at that time of night. It's past four by the time I make my way back out of town, and the petrol light flashes on before I get to the motorway. I wait for one of those posh garages, with the nice little shop in them and all, and when I spy one I pull into the forecourt. I get out and stretch me legs, no real hurry to get to pumping, got nowhere to be soon.

Forecourt is clean and well lighted, and I blink under the brightness of it. As I head round to take the cap off I nod to the man in the garage. He gives me a nod back as he turns the pump on, stretches out himself too. I fill the car up and wander to the night pay window, but he waves me round to the door. It's good to be out of the cold, and the place has one of those fancy coffee machines that are supposed to make it taste like you got it from a shop. I tell it to make me a large white one, and browse the shop while it hisses away. Grab a bunch of flowers from the bucket by the door and, after hearing my gut growl, a sandwich too.

'Just heading home?' the man at the till says as he starts scanning things. He looks a few years younger than me, early forties I'd say, and Indian, or at least from somewhere round there. Probably British these days, but you know what I mean. Sounded English enough.

'Sorry?' I say, digging the wallet from my back pocket.

'People, this time of night, either get coffee to stay awake for the day, or flowers for the way home. You have both.'

'Heading back home, I suppose,' I say.

'You work nights too?' he asked me; it was strange, but working overnight where he was must have been lonely. He was probably keen for the chat.

'For as long as I can remember.'

'I've only been doing it a few months. It's tough, perhaps I should bring back flowers after work as well, might make me more popular.'

'Got a family waiting?' I ask him, not too sure why but it's a nice break from the driving anyway. I take a sip of coffee; not too bad for a machine.

'Lovely wife. Two kids, one of each, both little, just starting school. My parents live with us too, so my wife has help with them, but I know she'd rather I be there to do it.'

'You got to work nights? I'm sure you'd rather be back home and all.'

'I would, but these shifts pay better. I used to do other things, better things, but times change, I suppose. If I do this now, my wife doesn't need to work. I do this for them. For now, that'll have to do. I'm sure you understand.'

I finish my coffee and wish the guy goodnight. I feel for him, working the lonely overnight. He may well have been one of the blokes who called in to the radio. They got that piped-in music in the shop, but he could have had a little something in there to listen on. Wish he'd understand, though, it's not what your family is about, or what you do for them. There's more to it than that, hard to put the words to. Don't think I realised it for a long time, but now I put the effort in. Got to.

I lay the flowers on the back seat and open the sarnie, eating half before I drive off. Sky starting to stain from blue-black to orange, few more cars on the road, streetlights not looking so bright as the world lights up. Morning's coming, new day. Head back onto the road, bit of spring in my step. Hate that bridging bit of time, too late to be night but too early to be morning, and feel good with the morning sun. Feel energised, like I'd slept all night, and get on with the driving.

The sun is low but bright when I get to the cemetery, sky clear for a nice dry day. I park up on the main street outside and grab the flowers out of the back of the car. It's properly cold, made all the worse with how bright the sun is this time of day, taunting you with how hot it should be. I put my coat on, pull the gloves out the pocket, and walk past the main gate. It's still chained this time of day, not supposed to let people in till nine, but I come here often enough I know the groundskeeper and he doesn't mind if I slip in through his gate. Knows I'm no trouble.

There's a thick frost on the ground, patches of fog hugging it close. It's peaceful, pretty too. The damp, cold smell gives it something like the feel of life. Smells fertile, like things start here as well as laying at rest. I recognise most of the plots as I go, walked this way for fourteen-odd years now. No new ones in this bit of the place. A few of them are well kept, most of them aren't. Groundskeeper does his bit for them, and with a few nearby my family I try to remember flowers for their birthdays and all. Nothing big, just get an extra bunch, but make sure they get something.

I walk off the path, satisfying crunch of frost cracking under me feet, over to Jenny and her mum. I open up the flowers and lay them out; Jenny always gets the bright coloured ones, and Alisha gets the lighter ones that she loved to leave around the house. I stuff the wrapping in my pocket and look at my family, smiling a little grin to myself.

'Morning, girls,' I say, fog from me breath floating away and joining the mist already hanging in the air above.

Dreamers

'You go on about this job,' Dad says to me, right as I get off the phone to my new bossman about starting, 'I can give you a job. I can talk to my friends, see if they can. Why this job?'

'I keep telling you,' I say back, practising my patience, 'I've worked in that warehouse of yours every school holiday since I was twelve.'

'Exactly, you know the business. It makes sense.' He has a big swig of brandy out of one of those Coke glasses they give away every now and then. Behind him, Mum starts chopping the veg for dinner a bit quieter.

'It's not going anywhere, though, is it?' I say. 'You can't pay me, you—'

'I let you live here. Roof over your head, food on the table.'

'I want my own money, don't I? Want to get my own roof.'

'My home isn't good enough for you?' Dad shouts.

'It's not like that, is it? Not what I mean. If I want to get a flat, some nice suits, move into central, I need money, don't I? Moving boxes around that warehouse of yours doesn't pay. I need more.'

'Bloody downright ungrateful fool,' he says. Behind him Mum's stopped all her chopping, looking back at us over her shoulder. Dad can't see her but I can, and I know her stare is all she can do to tell me to drop it, but I can't let it slide any more.

'Dad, I'm grateful, but we both said that if I hung around at school, got A levels, and worked for you on my time off, then if I didn't want to work at the warehouse I didn't have to.'

He finishes the rest of the brandy in a big gulp, the burn not registering with him, and bangs the glass down on the table. Mum jumps and turns back away.

'Bloody ungrateful. You know how embarrassing this is for me? I build up a business, train my only son in it, only to have him turn it down. Instead he wants to go on the high street, work for some bookies, taking bets from the kinds of people who go in there. All where anyone can see him. Pride sold for a few quid an hour.'

'It's not like that.'

'Of course it is. You can only be proud of your work if you do it for yourself.'

'That's not true, not here, not for me.'

'Feed you, clothe you, and now this.'

'I need money too, Dad.'

'There is no money any more. It's a recession.'

'The recession's over.'

All he does is rent a shitbox warehouse on the trading estate, storing stock for his makes with proper shops. Drives around a clapped-out Volvo to drop things off when they call him. 'Overstock Management Solution' he called it. It's not even a problem these days, what with stock run by computers and deliveries every day. Got no future to it, but he doesn't see that.

'Why not university, like your sister? Hmm? Do something respectable, become a dentist like her,' he says, not letting up. 'Work for me, then I'll pay for you to go too.'

Mum stops fussing over dinner and shoots me a look. This time I'll obey it. Dad doesn't know that my sister got a job to help her through uni. Mum helped her with that, but Dad thinks sis does it all through loans and the few quid he sends her. This time I obey Mum; don't want to open up that bucket of shit, and def don't want to fuck my sister over.

'I want to work, Dad. Get out, earn money. That's all.'

He goes on, and I listen until he's had his say. Knew I wasn't going to convince him, but I had to tell him. After a quiet dinner, Mum trying her best to get me and Dad chatting but not able to make much headway, I go to my room. Got to head into the new Paddy Power down on the high street early the next day. Paperwork to fill in, get shirts, pick up training books, that kind of thing. Work's starting.

Only takes me a few shifts to get into life down at Paddy Power. Little bit the same each day, but the pay adds up and it's good for a laugh. Had to get them to redo my name tag, they had me down as 'Mohammed' but I prefer just going by 'Mo', but otherwise it's alright.

Best part of it are the people. They come in crowds all day, each set acting like you're their best mate. Daytimes are mostly the blokes who work at the Indian round the corner. Fucking awful they are; must wager close to a ton a day, usually don't win. All horses and footie. On my first day they came in and started chatting to me in Hindi, thinking just 'cause I got the skin I can talk it. I don't have a bloody clue, but it's all blessed, we have a good laugh about it now. Only one who cared about learning that stuff was Grandma. Not even Dad wanted to carry on with all that, when she left so did chatting foreign. Still know how to swear in it, though. Standard.

Each afternoon you can set your watch by Malcolm coming in. Always dressed the same – shabby suits that went out of style in the eighties and don't quite fit him, covered up in a flasher's mac – and always with the same stupid chirpy attitude.

'Today's gonna be the day, Mo,' he'll always start, 'today is it. No more dreaming. Feeling lucky over here.'

'I believe in you,' I'll say back, something like that, got to play along, 'felt it when I woke up. It's going to be a good day.'

'Big win, this is the one, just you watch,' he'll say, slapping down a tenner and a bunch of slips. Thing is he never stands a chance. He does horses in the week, footie at weekends, building accumulators that are thousands, tens of thousands to one. It's a joke. You want the roulette crowd to see him, see what they'll be one day. There's a reason the shit he bets on has such high odds: you don't win. Never.

The lot I'm keen on actually getting matey with are from some office. Young lads, always the same two, third one changes every few weeks. Must work in central, not local. Probably in the new flats by the station or something. They meet at the shop after work, stick a bit on the horses, maybe a few quid in the roulette machines but they're smart about it all, then head down to the pub. They each always stick a tenner on the last race of the day, and when they pay their stakes they've got a shit-ton of notes in their wallets.

'What do you get up to when you get out of here?' one of them asks me after a few weeks, bored after busting out of a roulette machine. Know his name's Johnny, least that's what the lads call him, but he's never said anything to me so I feel all awkward actually calling him that.

'Not much, not much,' I say to him, trying to play it cool, 'get a bit of rest, back here early the next day. I work doubles most of the time. You know how it is, try and get ahead.'

'Get ahead, in here? Bloody hell,' Johnny says, shaking his head all exaggerated like. Yeah, it pisses me off, but I keep it cool.

'Not so bad, gotta start somewhere,' I say, before getting quieter to be sure that bossman in the back doesn't hear me, 'and it's not like I want to be a lifer here or nothing.'

'Still, I mean, don't want to be rude, but bloody hell . . . Hey, Matty,' Johnny calls out to one of the other lads, just finishing up on a machine. 'Mo here tells me that working in a place like this is getting somewhere in life. That can't be true, can it?'

'He's got something,' Matty says, looking down and a bit sheepish, not wanting to join in the game that Johnny's playing on me. He hands me a slip instead, and a horse had come in. He's got twenty quid on it at 5/1, so I pay him out a hundred and twenty. I know that the business isn't built on winners, that he loses more often than not, all that, but it still gives us a bit of a pang to pay out more than I'd earned all day to someone who had a lot more than me to start.

'Matthew, where's your heart?' Johnny starts up. Tone of his voice makes me sick but I don't say it. It's just a bit of banter anyhow, nothing worth getting steamed over. 'I bet our friend here works a lot harder than us.'

'Work smarter, not harder,' goes Matty, as he stuffs his cash into his wallet. The last forty is a tight squeeze, so he decides to put it in the roulette machine instead.

'Tell you what,' Johnny says to me, 'when do you get out of here?'

'About half an hour,' I say, little twinge of excitement.

'We'll be around the corner having a few drinks. Come by, we'll impart some wisdom on you.'

'Alright, sounds good. Round at The Falcon, yeah?'

'Christ, no. That dump? Only time any of us go in there is when Matty goes sport-fucking the locals. We'll be round at The Grange.'

Know the place. Not a big fan; over a fiver a pint. Still, I tell Johnny I'll see them there. Matty loses the cash he didn't put in his wallet, but the other young lad with them seemed to have won a bit and as they head out Johnny tells him that he's buying.

Bossman comes out from the back to take over on the till. We chat for a bit, nothing important, just a bit of training stuff, and after a while he says good job, same time tomorrow, all of that. I grab my things from the back room and shoot a text to Dad, saying something about needing to stay late and help set up some new display stuff for the next day. Feel bad for lying, but he'd not be happy if I was skipping out on dinner to go to the pub and it saved the aggro.

As I get close to The Grange I see Malcolm sitting on one of the benches which are dotted down the Quarry's sad excuse for a high street. He's on his tod, staring off down the road with a can of lager in his hand. I try to get my head down but he sees me.

'Thought you said I was having a lucky one today,' he says. Nothing in it but a bit of a joke, but I don't want to be seen walking down the street sharing a laugh with him.

'Must have been a bit off about today. Maybe tomorrow,' I say as I pass him. He lets out a laugh.

'"Yesterday is but today's memory, and tomorrow is today's dream,"' he says, and it makes me stop. Doesn't sound like the normal tripe he usually spews. I'm curious, but put my head down and keep on towards The Grange anyway. A few paces down the road I look back over my shoulder and he's looking down at his feet.

The Grange is all lit up nice in the evening. I stop for a bit, nerves getting the best of me. What if the office guys aren't having a bit of banter, what if they're having a laugh at me and they won't be there? Plus I'm dressed like shit compared to the rest of the crowd. I went in there for a mate's birthday once, only time I have, and it's well nice: dark wood and white walls, bits of art hanging which don't even look like anything. The brass on the bar is well polished, and everyone behind it dresses like they're from an old film or something, white shirts and waistcoats. I'm right out of place in scuffed work shoes, trousers and jumper from Tesco's, and underneath it all that stupid green shirt that work makes me wear. I push through it, though, got to take your chances when they come, and open the heavy glass and oak door. I spot the lads at the bar straight off, pints in hands. Johnny is holding court, and when he sees me he waves us over.

'Mo, good to see you, what're you drinking?' he says, friendly but no handshake. I'm not a big drinker, never got into it when a lot of the guys from school did. They'd head down The Falcon with their brothers' IDs to chance it, I'd normally be stuck working with Dad. Only thing I really knew was a brandy and Coke from when I lifted drinks from his stash, but I know you're supposed to follow the group with this stuff.

'I'm good with a Peroni, cheers,' I say, spying the logo on their glass.

'Good. Matty, it's your round,' Johnny says.

'Bullshit, it's yours,' Matty says, not happy.

'Yeah, but you had that nice little winner, didn't you. Only polite to share the wealth.'

'Wasn't that much, was it, Mo?' Matty says to me, and I'm feeling the pressure.

'Company policy,' I say, thinking nice and quick, 'can't say what people bet, won, or lost. He looks trustworthy enough, though.'

Get a good laugh from Matty and the other guy, but Johnny doesn't seem best pleased. He skulks off to the bar, and it hits that I probably should've sided with Johnny. He's a bit much, but looks like the one in charge. Don't have time to stew, as Matty introduces himself properly, as Matt. Shakes me by the hand, then introduces me to the lad with him. Calls him James and says he's a new hire, on trial with him and Johnny. Guy looks knackered, puffy eyes and a few stray hairs on his face that he's missed shaving. Before I can say hello to him Johnny shouts for a hand from the bar. I try to go over, make up for calling him out, but James is off like a whippet to help out. He comes back holding pints for himself and Matt. Johnny comes back over with two more and a glass of something brown.

'Get that down your neck,' he says to me, 'penalty for missing the first few rounds.'

He thrusts the small glass into my hand and I give it a quick sniff. It's whiskey, I reckon. Don't know what kind exactly, never really drink the stuff, but it smells enough of it. Bigger than you usually see poured, too. Johnny looks at me all expectant, wants me to chug it down no problem. That's not happening anytime soon, and instead I bring the glass to my mouth real timid and have a small sip. It tastes grim and burns real bad.

'The fuck was that?' Johnny says. 'Just get it down.'

Bit of panic creeps and I chuck the liquid into my mouth. Hadn't thought it through, and it sits on my tongue tasting awful and burning. Johnny's laughing at me as he knows I haven't swallowed it, and each second it sits there it looks less likely to go down. I take a big breath in through my nose and suck it down. As it hits my stomach it wants to come back up, but I hold on tight and concentrate on getting air in and out. When I turn to put the glass back on the bar I feel my eyes water up a bit, so I wipe them as quick and subtle as I can. That was fucking awful, and I can see Johnny laughing when I turn back. He hands me a beer anyway, though.

'Go down a bit funny, did it?' he says, rest of the guys following his lead with smirks.

'Rough way to start the night, is all,' I say, trying to play it off.

'Bad form to take it like you did, not very impressive.' Johnny seems real serious, and I got no clue if it's a part of the act. Need something else to drink bad; beer doesn't go down great, but I have a few slugs of it to try to stop the whiskey from coming back up. Kind of works, get my composure back at least, though Johnny still doesn't look too happy.

'So,' he chimes up, shooting a glance over to Matt before looking all business-like back at me, 'you're working down the bookies to get ahead?'

'Yeah, something like that,' I say, having to do a hard swallow before I speak to keep the drink down, 'trying to save a bit of money up, buy some suits, make sure I can get into town for interviews, that kind of thing.'

'You can cut all that shit out, I know what you mean. And keep pace, come on,' Johnny says, and I notice him and the other lads are well down on their beers while I've only had a bit.

'People don't work at bookies to "get ahead", we both know that,' he carries on, 'they do it to find out which horses are winning.'

'I just needed a job, that's all. This is all there was.'

'See,' he says, 'you're a natural gambler. Weren't even looking for it and you get yourself a peach of a gig.'

Don't know what he means really, but while I get to drinking he gets to talking. Says that the horses are dirty, owners will have a word with each other and mess with the odds. They'll put up a strong favourite who should win no trouble, and it'll push the rest of the field's odds up. Then they'll have the fave do a canter – say it was just a dummy run for the horse, or whatever – and one of the long odds horses'll win it. Johnny says that all the jockeys and owners are in on it, and they'll all have a bit of money on who they've chosen to win. I nod along; don't really know anything about that, but he's selling it alright. Get down to the dregs of my beer, not feeling great and glad it's over, but Matt takes the dead glass out my hand and slips in a fresh one. Rest of the guys have fresh ones too, so I have to say thanks and get going.

'Only way to get ahead,' Johnny says, big grin all over his head, 'is to know which ones are the fixed races. You get what I'm saying? You can do that, see where the money's going. You can tell us the horses that people are making moves on.'

He explains how to see it, watch the odds on an outsider horse tumble throughout the day as more and more money gets on it, until it winds up the new favourite. I've seen it happen a few times, I think. Maybe.

'All I need you to do,' he says, finale in his little pitch, 'is text me when you see it. That's all.'

'But I can't,' I say quickly, 'we had this talk when I started. Stuff like that, it's not allowed. Bad for business, cheating, get caught and I'll get the sack. Maybe worse.'

Don't know why I shot it down like that. Think it's that it's not real legal; I get a record for something like that, I can kiss a good job goodbye. Drink's affecting me. Maybe it's just that. Feel funny, like I'm sat back in myself, watching what's going on through my own eyes.

'Oh, come off it,' Johnny says, ''course they try and scare you off; if punters win they lose money. But what've they ever done for you? Given you a green shirt and six quid an hour?'

'It's better than I had before. I need that job.'

'Alright then,' he says, making a right show of it, 'how about this, then. You keep an eye on the odds for us, and you be smart and send me a text when you see a goer. They'll never know it's you sending out tips, you're not staking anything. Get us a few winners, and I'll see if I can sort you out with a trial at our place. That London job you want so bad. Everyone wins.'

I start nodding. Want all that, but don't know what I'd do if it all went tits up. Back to Dad and the warehouse, so cold you've got to wear a jacket inside in the winter?

'What's the job' I ask, but feel the words come out thick and strange from my mouth. Must be drunk. Got to hold it together. There's a fresh pint in my hand.

'Recruitment consultancy,' Johnny says, looking proud, 'easy work if you're on the ball. Get a lot on trial, like young James here is at the minute. It's tough, but you don't need much training: people skills, hard work, eye for talent. There's money if you're willing to put the hours in.'

Don't know what to think. Thought I'd do anything for that chance, but if I get sacked from my first proper job for cheating, that's it. I'd be done. My life'd be driving Dad's Volvo around with cans of soup in the boot, while he drinks a bottle of Coke he thinks I don't know has brandy in it.

'Let me think,' I say. Can't take it in right now. Head's gone. Johnny grins anyway. 'Good lad, smart lad, good to think it over,' he says. Hands me a card with his name and number on it, tells me to text him when I've had a think.

'Let's celebrate like you've said yes anyway,' he says, hard pat on my back. 'Your round, I'll help you carry.'

Stumble in the front door and I feel like death. It's late – squinting at my watch it looks to say about eleven, but that's a guess at best – and the lights are off. The strong smell of turmeric and cumin from dinner churns my stomach. Just want to have a slash and go to sleep. I bounce off the walls on the way to the toilet, and when I'm done go to do the same on the way to my bedroom.

'Mohammed, come here,' I hear Dad shout from the kitchen. He's slurring as bad as I reckon I am.

'Can't it wait, Dad? Got work early,' I say, eyes closed and leaning on the wall.

'Here. Now,' he shouts, louder, banging at the table. Fucksake.

Take a big breath and do my best to make it down the hallway in one piece. Get a tilt on and fall, though, knocking a picture against the wall and drop to a knee. Dad shouts again and I right myself. Make it into the kitchen, barely.

'Sit,' he says, pointing at a chair. Dad's still in his work clothes, bottle of brandy mostly gone and a chipped pink tea mug in front of him. I do what he says, can't be bothered with trouble.

'Where've you been?' he asks.

'Stayed late at work,' I mumble. See the tap over the sink dripping. Water sounds like bliss right now.

'Bullshit, liar,' he says, taking a big sup from his mug.

'Stayed late, that's all.'

'You're drunk.'

'I mean, yeah. But no, went to the pub after work with the bossman, yeah. That's all.'

'Drunk. You're drunk,' he says, real snarl to it. He pulls the top off the brandy bottle and throws another slug into his mug.

'What do you want? What do you want me to say?' I ask.

He's shut up and I stand to go get a water. I have to do it real slow to make sure I don't topple, but I manage it.

'Where are you going?' he shouts.

'Get a water, alright?'

'Back down,' he says, pointing at the chair. I flop, somehow not stacking it as I do.

He's furious but I just want this done and over.

'My friends, they make fun of me,' he says. 'My son, my only son, wants to work on the high street in a, in a bookmaker's. Doesn't want to go into business with his father.'

Fucksake. Feel like shit, just want to go to bed.

'The day my father asked me to join him in his business, proudest day of my life. It's an honour, to work for the family. Taught me how to start my own business, provide for my own family.'

And a real good job you do at that, don't you? Man's a joke. I stare past him, shoot daggers at the cupboard.

'I send my daughter to university. I make sure my wife

doesn't have to work. But I raise an ungrateful son who disrespects me.'

He stops to take a big drink.

'Rather than learn about the world from his father, than help grow a business, he sits on the high street with – with – degenerates, for all of the world to see. Taking bets and coming home drunk. A drunk.'

'Fuck off, you're the drunk,' I say before I can catch the words coming out of my face.

His eyes meet mine, and before I can say something to backtrack his body snatches. He picks up the mug and chucks it at my head. It hits flush, right above my right eye, and it fucking kills. Doesn't break on my head, but it bounces off and smashes against the cupboards behind. Force of it unsettles me and I go sprawling, land right on my hip, but I'm more worried about cradling my face. There's blood on my hand from where it's split my eyebrow.

'Don't you fucking disrespect me,' he yells, standing over me. He whacks me round the back of the head for good measure.

'Fuck, I'm sorry, alright? Just slipped out,' I say, for the fat lot of good it'll do.

'I should throw you out. I only don't because it would make me look worse.'

He steps back and I find a bit of floor without shattered ceramics all over it to put down a hand and push myself up. I keep my head down and walk, best as I can, down the hall towards my room, the shock of it all keeping me upright.

'Don't turn your back on me, I didn't say you could go,' Dad shouts after me, but I keep moving. I hear him start to make his way out of the kitchen and down the hall too, so I dive into my room and shut the door. No lock on it, Dad never let us have them, but I lean up against it. Feel my eyebrow and it's got a bit of a lump, blood still trickling. No idea if it needs stitches, but no chance of getting a lift to the hospital or anything. Hip is really starting to ache.

Dad pounds on the door, yelling at me to get out and face him, and it jolts me. Didn't say anything back, just kept braced against the door best as my hip would let me, to stop him.

'Let him be,' I hear my mum say softly from the other side of the door. He'd better not start on her. I tighten my hand on the doorknob.

He keeps going on about disrespect, but I can hear Mum trying to soothe him, apologising for me – 'He's been working late, he didn't mean it,' and, 'He's just been out with friends, it's good for a boy his age' – before she coaxes him away. He leaves with a big smack on the door as a grand finale of a 'fuck you', and I feel the thing shift as it loosens the hinges. He carries on as Mum leads him to their room, and I stay pressed against the door as I hear the rough rumble of his shouts go through the house. Once I'm sure he's not going to be busting in I grab the old dining room chair I use as a desk chair and wedge the back of it up against the door handle. Don't know if it'd actually work and stop him getting in if he gets riled up during the night, but it'd make a big enough racket to wake me up.

Sun comes up to the worst morning of my life. Must've passed out soon as I was done with the chair, and wake up fully clothed on the bed, pillow stuck to my face where the cut had caught the fabric of it in the scab. Head's pounding and I'd been sick in the night, a trail of the putrid stuff going over the side of the bed and onto the floor. No idea if it's from the drink or the whack I had. I squint my eyes at my watch and it looks like it says nine-thirty. Sit up quick as my body'll allow and look at the alarm clock I never set. It confirms it. Should have been at work half an hour ago. I grab my phone from my pocket but it's dead. Try to stand but the only thing killing more than my head is my hip, like I'm being stabbed, knife rolling around in the joint. I want to shuffle along the bathroom for a shower but I'm real cautious opening the door. Don't want to run into Dad, but it looks like nobody's home. In the shower I see my hip showing shades I didn't know bodies made. When I close my eyes to shampoo my hair, the world spins and I start dry heaving.

I'm well over an hour late when I roll up to work. Must've looked a right state doing a running limp down the high street to get there. Cut had closed up again, though, so at least I didn't do it bleeding. Probably did need stitches, but don't have time for that now. I push the door to the shop open real timid, already saying my sorries, and the bossman starts to ask where I've been all morning before lifting his head to look at me.

'Bloody hell, Mo, you okay?' he asks.

'Yeah, yeah, I'm fine. I'm really sorry for being late,' I say, expecting the bollocking.

'Don't worry about it. You sure you're alright? What happened?'

Shit. Hadn't thought about that.

'Playing football with some mates,' I say before I think it through, ignoring that he could have seen me in the pub, and that it's winter, and that I got out of work well after dark, all that shit, 'went for a big volley, forgot the ground was still so hard. Bit of a knock in the air, and stacked it.'

I give a bit of a laugh, play through the actions best I can with my gammy leg, tried to sell it.

'Bashed my head,' I carry on, 'forgot to set an alarm last night, slow-moving this morning. I'm sorry.'

He tells me not to worry, asks if I want the day off to rest up at home. Tell him I don't. It's not half an hour into the shift before I sneak a text off to Johnny telling him I'm in.

Takes me a week or so to spot my first horse. Another to find the second. I text Johnny the heads-up when they still have their long odds, both over 10/1. By the time they race they're odds-on, and each night Johnny is beaming when he comes in. Doesn't invite me out again to celebrate or nothing, but guessing he just doesn't want to be suspicious.

I don't see Dad, though. It's just me and Mum at dinner for weeks. I hear him come home late, when I'm already in my room. I don't go out to talk to him and he doesn't come to my door to talk to me. I catch a glimpse of him once. I'd been practising drinking sometimes, sneaking a four pack of beer home after shifts and seeing how quick I could get them all down, but it made me need to piss like nothing. One night I have to go while he's still in the kitchen eating the plate Mum kept warm for him, but even though he must hear me he doesn't look up.

Another week or two, another winner or two, and I'm thinking I should ask Johnny about that trial. I've got a bit of cash saved up, enough for the trains and some nicer clothes. Might be time. James had stopped turning up with them, replaced with a new young lad who they didn't introduce me to, so James'd either made it or hadn't. Probably hadn't, he was quiet. I could do a better job than him, knew I could.

Another Dad-less week goes by and I think I spot another horse. I text Johnny from the backroom at work, and before I walk back out to the front of the shop I hear my phone go off. I check it, and it's the message bounced back, undeliverable. I try it again, same deal. I know the number's right, I can see the ones he's got fine on the screen. I want to try calling but there are people waiting out front.

I'm behind the counter with the bossman when Matt comes in with the new recruit and heads straight back to the roulette machines. No Johnny in sight. I keep trying to catch their eye but they aren't looking. When they come up to the desk to put their horse bet on, they deal with bossman, have a laugh with him, and I'm stuck with Malcolm.

'Late evening luck rush,' he says to me, 'gonna send me to bed happy.'

'Yeah, yeah,' I say, trying more to listen in to whatever Matt was saying. 'You're not feeling it today?' Malcolm says.

'Lucky? Yeah. 'Course. Always.'

'Don't seem it. Got to keep dreaming.'

I nod and smile at him, not giving the tiniest of shits. I run his ticket into the machine, and it's another typical

Malcolm bet: couple of horses, big stake, bigger odds, no chance. Except one of the horses he's backing is in the same race as the one I tried to give Johnny a tip about earlier.

'Really don't know about this one, Malcolm,' I say, quiet, so the boss doesn't hear. We're not exactly in the business of discouragement.

'Come now, Mo,' he says, real dramatic, 'I thought you had more faith than that.'

'You sure about Coffee Bean?' I say about the horse he's got that I know isn't winning.

''Course he is, he's a little dream maker,' Malc says, and I can't do nothing else.

'I think you should go with someone else,' I tell him.

'I know what I'm doing,' Malc says. I've never seen him angry before, and he scratches up his face all indignant.

'C'mon mate, I don't want to see you lose is all.'

'Lose? What makes you think I'm going to lose?' He's getting loud, bossman looks over.

'Nothing, just a feeling about that horse is all. Feels like a bad race to back.'

'I know what I'm doing, you stupid boy,' Malc says to me, loud. 'Show a bit of respect. That's all I want, is that so hard for you, hmm?' he says, real theatrical.

'Alright, sorry, yeah,' I say and run his ticket. Maybe I got this one wrong. Hope I did. Malcolm doesn't stay at the counter to chat like usual, though. He buries his slip into his grubby mac pocket and storms to a table in the corner to watch the race. The bossman asks me what's up and I shrug at him. Tell him Malc must've had a bad day, and he accepts it.

I keep busy, fussing behind the desk at pens and papers

while Matt goes to the back with the new recruit to have round two on the roulette machines. I walk into the back room and back out, just trying to see if he looks up, but he doesn't. Have to wait until he's leaving, still not looking at me, and hiss to get his attention.

'Matt,' I say quiet, not wanting the bossman in the back to hear me, 'Matt.' He doesn't do anything to respond.

'Matt, hold up,' I say, and he sighs as he stops. He doesn't want to talk and I'm bricking it. I hear him tell the new guy with him to wait outside.

'Mo, listen,' he says, gingerly leaning over the counter, 'maybe we need a chat. You finish soon, yeah? Meet us down The Grange real quick when you're done.'

I nod and he walks off. Get a massive fizz of anxious. Something's going down. I was an idiot, shouldn't have sent Johnny anything. Malcolm's horse doesn't come in, the tip I knew was good did, and I watch him as he drains the last of his tin and scrunch it up. He's got two more races on his ticket but the bet's dead, so he puts it along with the can into the bin and leaves. Should have given it to him. He deserves it.

Soon as the bossman comes to say it's time I can head out I bolt to the back to get my stuff. Usually I try and hang around a bit, have a chat with the boss, keep him sweet, but not today. I'm straight out and hotfoot it to the pub. Malcolm's on his bench, fresh set of beers, but I don't give him the chance to slow me down today.

I cool it as I get towards the pub so I don't turn up out of breath, and it takes me a while of scanning the room to spot Matt. Probably look like a nutter, wide-eyed and head spinning around, but I don't care as I dart through the various tables and bodies between me and him.

'Matt, hi, how are you?' I splutter out when I get to him, holding out a hand which he gives a limp, passing shake to. 'Can I get you a beer? Do you want a beer? How about—'

'Mo, hold up,' he says, and he pulls a pack of cigarettes from his pocket, 'head outside with me.'

Matt asks the new lad to keep their spot and hang on to his beer before leading me through to the back garden smoking place. It's proper nice out there: fancy deck, big plants, tables nicer than what we got at home. Matt lights a cigarette and doesn't offer me one.

'I tried to text Johnny some stuff today,' I say, 'but the number's dead.'

'Look, Johnny got the sack end of last week,' he says, exhaling his first drag.

'That's a shame,' I say, but can feel my face crease up in nerves. Sacked for what? 'He was a nice bloke.'

'Oh, don't be so fuckin' thick,' Matt spits, 'the guy was a wanker and bent as anything. It all caught up with him in the end.'

'So it wasn't about the – you know – what we did, the horses, then?' I ask, hushed voice. For a split second, stupid as it sounds, it actually makes me feel important; hushed chats about business gone wrong.

'Nah. He never shared the tips anyway. Just liked to show off the wedge and tell people that he had a guy in the industry, all to big himself up. Tosser.'

'Right. Okay. So what now, though, because he said, like—' I begin to ask. Know I should speak up for myself but Matt's the most pissed at Johnny. Don't exactly think he wants to go around settling Johnny's debts for him.

'Look, he dangles that carrot out for anyone desperate or stupid enough for it to get him what he wants.'

I wait for him to say 'no offence' but he doesn't.

'It was his biggest scam, the one that got him caught,' Matt carries on. 'We got open, rolling recruitment at work. It's kind of bullshit, high turnover, sink or swim, no training, that kind of thing, but whatever. If we refer someone, they swim, they make money and do well, we get a cut. It's how it works. Johnny would use that referral to milk whatever he could out of people, then stop giving a shit and send them to the same open interviews they could get off the street. He got what he wanted, and if they did well they just earned him more money.'

'Right,' I say. Should I have known? 'Course I should.

'Anyway,' Matt says, finishing off his cig and stubbing it into a giant green glass ashtray, 'I'm sorry for how he was. Think we're going to shake up our after-work routine a bit now, you know. Probably won't come around as often.'

He gives a little nod as a goodbye and walks past me. So that's it? Risk my job, fall out with my dad, goodbye to getting out of here anytime soon, all for that? Bollocks to it.

'Matt, you said open recruitment,' I say. He turns around, not looking keen.

'Look, Mo, I don't know if that's too much of a good idea. It's a different world from round here, and—'

'Don't refer me if you don't want to,' I say, me actually cutting him off, 'but tell me when and where.'

Matt leans his head back and blows out through his nose.

He reaches into his pocket to grab another snout, and as he drops the lighter back in he pulls out a pen and business card. He leans onto one of the dryer tables and jots down some details.

'Look, if you really want to, here. Go to the website, put me in as a referral, and someone'll let you know when the next round of recruitment is. Won't be more than a few weeks. Be early, get a nice suit, and don't mention Johnny. Don't mention me. Just pretend you found it online or something, alright?'

With that he shoves the card in my hand and walks off, not giving us a chance to ask him anything else. And I'm actually pretty happy. I got it, an in. Yeah, it's not ideal, not going to have anyone putting in a friendly word with their boss for me, but it's still an in. And I don't buy Matty's bitterness, anyway. I'm sure Johnny saw something in me. He might have just got a promotion, maybe a better job with a better company, and Matty's bitter because Johnny went up and he's still stuck where he was. If Johnny got a plum gig with a rival, they'd cut his phone off. Stop him taking all his contacts.

I leave The Grange by their garden exit and have a little spring in my step. I can get online, fill the form out tonight, buy a suit on my next day off, keep pulling in the Paddy Power cash until the interview, then it's off to central. This is it. I walk home pretty happy, and it's only when the key's in the door that I realise I'm late for dinner. Not worried as Dad hasn't been in for dinner since he lugged that mug at my head, but feel bad for making Mum wait.

'Sorry,' I say as I kick my shoes off and head into my

room to put a non-work shirt on, 'got held up with something after work. What's for dinner?'

Except when I get into the kitchen Mum's not there. No sign of her. It's just Dad, sat at the table, half-full bottle of Tesco's own-brand brandy and a glass. No ice, no mixer. I brick it.

'Dad, sorry, I, uh—' I garble out.

Dad looks up at me, eyes glazed, bit red, and back down at his glass. He takes a huge swig, two gulps of neat brandy. Doesn't even flinch.

'Y'alright, Dad?' I say, real cautious. Man might be a joke, but still.

'Stupid. What a stupid, stupid thing to do,' he says.

'Okay,' I say, and turn to head back to my bedroom. Not in the mood for another of his drunk lectures.

'Not you, it's not always about you,' he shouts, and it stops me.

'Okay,' I say.

'I was fine to drive. Fine. Not a problem.'

'What happened?' I ask, gently, easing myself into the seat that he hit me off the last time I sat across from him a few weeks back. Getting this close he looked different; gaunter in the cheeks, but still bloated. He hadn't shaved in a while, and his eyes were well off, strange mix of red and yellow. His hair was messier, longer, and the grey roots he dyed tyre-black to cover were showing.

'They said I swerved a bit, pulled out in front of a car. It's bullshit. Because I'm Indian. Because I'm trying to get ahead. That's all it is.'

'What happened, Dad?'

'Made me take that stupid test. Said I'd been drinking, said I shouldn't drive. I told them I was fine but they didn't care. Took my car. Took everything in it. Took me to the station. They're going to take away my licence.'

He finally got caught out, then. Only a matter of time.

'If they take everything, then what?' he says. 'Can't drive, can't run the business. Can't do a thing. I'll be left a sad old man. A failure.'

'C'mon, Dad,' I say, 'it's not that bad.'

'What else is there? Your sister is off at university. Your mother is visiting her for a while. You've nearly left too. It's all gone,' he says.

He starts crying. Dad. Actually crying. Starts off little, him struggling to control his breathing, wiping his eyes like he's confused as to why they're wet. He shouts at himself as it gets worse, taking the glass to his mouth before slamming it back down and jamming both palms into his eyes.

'I could always drive, a bit,' I say quietly, soft enough he wouldn't hear it over his hurt.

'You want London,' he says, not looking at me.

'London will be there later.'

'You can't even drive.'

'I've been saving up a bit, haven't I? Could get some lessons.'

'You'd do that?'

'Yeah,' I say, 'why not?'

'You don't want that.'

We sit in silence. Dad takes another drink, this one barely a sip, and grimaces at it.

'Mum's with sis?' I ask after a while.

'Said she just wanted to see how she was,' Dad says. 'Help her. Exam time, final year. Big time. She'll be back.'

'Okay,' I say.

'I knew we'd drive her out,' he says, then, quietly. I nod. Makes sense. We were at it at dinner every night for months, then wouldn't be in the same room. Who'd want to put up with us.

'Maybe it's good if I help out a bit, then,' I say.

'I still have time before court. They need a judge to take my licence away. I can drive until then.'

'I could learn to drive.'

'Insurance will be high. You're young.'

'I can keep working until then. Get more money to get set up.'

'Okay,' he says after a pause.

'Okay,' I say too, settling my fate.

We sit in silence a bit longer, uneasy. I'm starving, but Dad says he isn't, so I tell him I'm going to pop out and get something. He nods, not looking up but keeping fixed on the brandy in front of him.

I pull on a thick hoodie and walk down the high street. There're some fast food places still open, but I go past them. I keep going, down through the park in the middle of the Quarry and then back again on the other side of the street. I keep walking, plod of my feet drowning out what I just agreed to. I walk past The Grange, lit up in the night, and look in the window. I can see Matt and the other lad still in there, joined by a few others, all laughing and joking. Think about going in to have a beer, casual like I just do that sometimes, but can't. That's not my world, don't know what I'm even doing trying to get into it. Instead I keep my head down, think about heading towards The Falcon, see if anyone I might know is still around. Could try and bump into them or something.

Walking down the high street Malcolm's still there on his bench, sat hunched over and holding a tinny. It's late, cold, and I hope he wasn't sleeping there. Never occurred to me that he might. I want to keep walking but owe him an apology.

'Y'alright, Malcolm?' I ask him, and he looks up.

'Not a lucky day today, Mo,' he says, looking off.

'Know the feeling. Look, mate, I'm sorry about earlier, yeah?'

'Forget it. You were right about that horse. Perhaps I should take your advice more.'

'I wouldn't,' I say. I should keep going, still got my old job to work in the morning, but I don't budge.

'You doing alright, Mo?' Malcolm asks, and I fidget. Don't know what to feel.

'Yeah. Sort of. Strange one, today, you know?' I say.

'Just got to keep dreaming,' he says.

'Be real. It's not bloody like that, Malc, is it?'

Malcolm laughs, little at first, but then louder and losing his senses a bit, all weird like earlier. I bounce on me heels and think about scarpering. Don't want to be seen with him like this, and he looks a bit mad anyway.

'Beer?' he says, wiping a tear off his cheek before reaching into the thick blue plastic bag down at his feet. It's one of those strong ones he drinks.

'Shouldn't.'

'Come on,' he says, and I take it. Truth is I could do with a drink. I wipe the top of it down with my sleeve and sit on the bench next to him. When I crack it open and take a sip it burns and tastes like shit, but after practising drinking I can take it now.

'You got to keep on dreaming, Mo,' he says, and I'm deaf to it.

'It's not like that, though,' I say again, taking an angry swig, 'I want things. Need to do more than dreaming. Need to work hard, get my shit together, get ahead, all of that. It's not about dreaming. Got to have your dreams, but you need to do shit about 'em.'

'What is it you want, then?'

'I want to be fucking out of here? Is that so much to ask? I want money. I want a decent job. I want to move to London on a good pay. I want to go out, chat to girls, fool about. Meet one, go from two shitty flats to one decent one. Get ahead at work, get money, get out of London and have kids. Wear jumpers over collared shirts when you walk your dog to the pub. Have an Aston on a gravel drive. Just fucking everything that isn't terrace houses, cheap beer, and bullshit jobs.'

'And what?' he says. 'Work every minute of your life in the hope you get some of that?'

'How else you gonna get it?'

'You got to dream, Mo,' he says again, stupid smile on his face showing cracked teeth.

'Dreaming don't get you there, though.'

'That's where you're wrong,' he says, smiling like the idiot he is. 'Gamblers are dreamers,' he says again, 'we believe your whole life can turn around in a second. Don't matter what you've done before, what you're doing now, it's that faith, that dream, your whole life can come good in an instant. Everything you want, instantly. Big bet, get an Aston. Big bet, get the money to get any girl to drop her dress. Won't even need that fancy London job. People piss their whole lives away, say it's all working hard, and most don't get shit back for it. That's not dreaming, that's surviving. We dream, Mo. We dream.'

He's pleased with himself but I look ahead and finish the can. It goes down quick and I got no dinner in me so my head spins a bit. I crush it and throw it into the bin beside our bench. Malcolm doesn't say anything else and neither do I. Instead I reach into my trouser pocket and look at the business card Matt gave me, throwing that in the bin too, and I sit and listen to the late-night sounds of home, the sirens in the background and shouts from the pubs.

Central

'Let me tell you something about Jap girls,' Briscoe says, leaning back in his chair as he takes a drink, watching the win from the slot machine get added to his balance, 'they fuck different to normal girls, ya know?'

'Can't really say that I do, mate,' I go, leaning back to drain the last of my drink so bad the ice nearly falls out over my face. Really not in the mood to hear his latest stories about sport-fucking around the world.

'Fuckin' weird, bruv, let me tell you that. Over here they're all normal, you know, like "ooo ooo ooo, Daddy, fuck me harder", but over there, man, it's like you're fuckin' breaking them or some shit like that. Ya know, all crying like they're in pain and shit. But they're fucking loving it, Nick, you know. It's weird, man. Fucking great too.'

I laugh and nod along but don't know what he's on about. Seen stuff like that in porn, but no idea what it's like in real life. Thought it was an act, like the operatic American shit.

I thumb at the slot machine in front of me and watch the money that Briscoe had loaned me for the night dwindle with each spin. Can't get a win from anywhere, and next to me Briscoe has doubled up. I don't know if he even realises he's up; seems more interested in keeping an eye on the girls on their nights out and waitresses to get more drinks from.

We're upstairs at the Empire Casino in central, right in Leicester Square. Normally I avoid going to places like this like the plague but Briscoe said he was paying tonight as I hadn't seen him in a while so I came. Plus I know there was no chance that he was heading back to the Quarry; he got out of there thanks to the navy long ago. He's been in Singapore on his last deployment for the past few years, working and travelling.

The Empire's a nice casino, way better than those cheap slot parlours you mostly get around my way. It's all glass and metal and light wood, lit real bright so everything shines. We're sat on the upper level playing on the slot machines, looking down on the action of the main casino floor. Below us men are in nice suits and women in tight dresses which cling around them, a tiny thinness of fabric covering what most of the men in the room would kill to see. I'm a bit glad we're away from all that. All I've got to wear is an old suit from Dad's funeral a few years back, and it's not fitting great. I've put on even more weight since then. I'm glad to be out of sight.

Briscoe must've ordered more drinks as two more Jack and Cokes arrive. He gives the waitress, a sexy black girl with elaborately tied-up braids, a fiver tip and says something which makes her break into a wide smile. She doesn't look at me.

'Thanks for the invite again,' I say as he passes me over a drink, 'can't remember the last time I really got out of town and into central.'

'No problem. Sorry myself for not coming back down your neck of the woods, but there is zero fuckin' chance I'm going back there for as long as I can help it. Plus, this isn't too much of a bad alternative.'

As he's chatting away, two girls with short dresses and naughty smiles walk by and grin at Briscoe. He gives smirks at them and raises his glass. They giggle to each other before disappearing through the frosted door into the high roller VIP area. I look back to my machine and lose another spin.

'Nice to get checked out when you're not in uniform, bruv, you know?' he says to me, like I'd have a clue. 'Over there, being in uniform is a fuckin' pussy magnet. Girls just love it. I'm telling you, man, being in the military is the best damn lie I ever told, and it's all fuckin' true to boot. You wear the gear and everyone assumes you're a fuckin' hero, fresh back from knocking off pirates around the seven seas or some shit like that. They don't ever stop to think all you've done is oversee a few repairs and fuck the natives.'

One of the girls comes back out from the frosted door on her phone. While she's talking she makes eyes at Briscoe again, who I catch smiling back.

'So, how is the old estate?' he asks when she goes back through the door.

'Same as when you sailed off.'

'That bad, huh?'

'I mean it isn't all so bad. Easy enough to get by.'

'Still can't believe you call that place home for real, man. Thought you'd be straight fucking out behind me.'

'Thought about it, but in the end it wasn't for me. Wouldn't have really flown through the physical like you.'

Briscoe nods. He used to give me the whole speech about how with a bit of work I could start shifting the weight, bit more school I could have done well on the technical side of things, but he's given up the last few times I've spoken to him.

'Still doesn't mean you couldn't have gotten out another way. It's dead easy to do uni these days, get trade, whatever.'

'It's not all that simple.'

'Sure it is. You can become a nurse for pretty much free as there's fuck all left of them, then you can go anywhere you want in the country.'

I look down and want to tell him that it's only people who've managed to get out who seem to think that getting out is so damn simple. Or worse, like with Briscoe, that it was simple for him so he assumes it'll be simple for everyone if they just tried or some shit like that. Just because he was smart and athletic and lucked into a cushy navy job doesn't mean we'd all find it that easy, and I wish he'd cut it out in thinking everyone who was still in the Quarry was a fuck-up.

Don't say that, though, do I? Instead I just give my pathetic little head a shake and have some of my drink.

'I'm sorry, mate,' Briscoe says, slapping a hand hard on my shoulder and holding it there for a few seconds before moving it back to spin the slots. 'I get it, London isn't the easy money it used to be, there's tuition fees for uni now, no factories or shit like that any more. And you've got to work harder and cheaper than the fuckin' Poles and Pakis. I know it can't be easy.'

Looks like he's still giving advice, just it's got a bit more complex than 'lose weight and your life will become hunky-fuckin'-dory'. I wish he'd shut up and move on, and as I'm looking at him I see his face completely change. It goes from a crumpled look of concern at me to wide eyes on the machine in front of him, mouth gawping shock. He's letting out little laughs and swearing to himself.

The screen is flashing one word: JACKPOT!

Briscoe shouted encouragement to the machine as the balance kept going up, the chimes ringing loud. A few people began to look over to us and Briscoe started doing a little dance. The display went on for five minutes, and by the time the machine quietened back down it was clear he'd hit the house jackpot.

The balance at the top of the screen read £10,000.

'Oh fuck, yes, fuckitty fuck, yes,' Briscoe shouts, violently hitting his hand off my back. It hurts like hell but he's excited and I let it go. 'Fucking hell, yeah. I knew coming into central was the right call, absolutely knew it. It's going to be a good night tonight, Nicky boy.'

'I can't believe it,' I say, 'ten grand, just like that?'

That's more than I clear a year with my part-time jobs and benefits, won by pressing a button on the machine next to the one I chose to sit at.

Fucksake, man.

Briscoe starts bashing the payout button but the machine is telling him to wait for an assistant. He gets anxious – says you hear about this kind of thing, casinos not paying out jackpots because of claims of a computer fault – before a little man in a suit comes over. He introduces himself as the shift manager that day.

'Congratulations,' he says, 'that's a nice win. With a jackpot win we do need to do a little paperwork, would you mind coming through to the VIP area while we go through things?'

Briscoe has gone full Cheshire Cat, nodding his head and feeling like he's in the big time.

'Absolutely,' he says, 'lead the way.'

'Excellent,' says the little manager, 'please follow me. We'll find you a table and something to drink while we go through things.'

I cashed out what was left of the hundred I'd put in the machine when me and Briscoe had started playing. There was £40.27 left.

'I'll catch up with you,' I say to Briscoe, 'going to pop out front and have a cigarette.'

While they go through the frosted glass door where the girls from earlier had been, I push my way through the crowd until I'm standing in Leicester Square. When I'm out there it's postcard London; neon signs and heavy foot traffic despite it being nearly midnight, faces and voices from all across the world swarming about together. There is peace in the late-night bustle, and away from the lights and the action and the girls in their dresses I can feel anonymous again. I like it. I can think, and can't shift the thought that in a fifty-fifty situation of picking one of two machines, of course it's Briscoe who picks the one which'll pay out ten grand.

As I'm finishing up my cigarette, two Asian girls – Japanese I think, from their dress – look around holding a mobile as if they're looking for somebody to take a picture of them. I could swear they look at me, sat quietly on a bench, before deciding to take an awkward selfie.

I smoke a second and head back upstairs to the VIP area to track down Briscoe. I don't get stopped as soon as I step through the frosted door, bit of a surprise, but feel the eyes of the room on me. Everyone here is thin and wealthy and laughing and I'm in an old, ill-fitting suit I only bought on the cheap to have something to bury Dad in. I hate it already.

I walk towards the bar and look around, wondering if Briscoe has done a runner or something. I check my phone, half expecting to find a text saying that he'd taken the money and a girl and was sorry, but there's nothing. It's when I walk towards the bar that I see him, sat pleased as punch in a booth by himself. On the table there's a bottle of something in an ice bucket, along with pitchers of Coke and a bucket of Red Bull.

When he clocks me he smiles and holds his arms out wide, before starting to fix me a drink from our private bar.

'They must think we're fucking stupid,' he says as he pulls a magnum of Grey Goose out of the ice bucket in front of us and begins pouring.

'What do you mean? This is sick, man. Didn't you buy all this?'

'C'mon, Nick, don't be so naïve. I didn't shell out for all this, the house laid it on while I waited for them to pay out. And it isn't nice of them, this is them wanting us to get fucked up and give them that money back.'

'Nah, man, maybe they're just trying to give us a good night.'

He hands me a vodka and Coke poured strong. I can't remember when I last drank vodka, and it tastes like shit to me, but Briscoe's having the time of his life and I don't want to rain on his parade. I take another sip, sucking it down before I can really taste it, before pouring some more mixer in.

'No chance,' Briscoe says, 'that isn't how this works. They're pissed that I got some of their money, 'cause they don't like it when people get their money. They don't earn that way. So what they're banking on is we drink this vodka, get drunk, then hit the tables up here in the high stakes area. Hope that we'll piss their money back at them, and we're happy with the story of how we won and lost ten grand in the VIP area of a casino one night while feeling like fuckin' kings. We'll think we won, but all we'll have is a hangover and the memory of holding a stack of cash. They'll have the only thing that matters.'

'Whatever you say,' I tell him, still not used to the unfamiliar vodka burn. I can feel it creeping up my chest.

'You know it's true. But we're not giving them the satisfaction. You know what this money really is? It's not life-changing, nah, but it's a chunk off the mortgage, can mod my car a bit, stay in nicer places on shore leave and it's a new TV so big I can't watch the whole screen at the same fuckin' time. It's a bit of freedom is what it is, and fuck them if they think I'll give it back because they gave me a bottle of vodka. I got a better plan.'

I want to ask what the fuck Briscoe's on about but he's absolutely buzzing and ranting and raving in his own little world. He pours himself another vodka and Red Bull before a smirk creeps across his face. Sat up at the bar, drinking colourful cocktails, are the two girls in short dresses who'd smiled at him earlier. One of them looks over her shoulder and when their eyes meet both Briscoe and the girl start grinning. Briscoe gives them a little wave to come over, and I watch as the two girls look at each other, share a laugh, before carefully sliding down off their bar stools to make sure their dresses don't slide up. As they walked over he kept his eyes on them, that same shit-eating grin on his face, before pouncing once they were close.

'Ladies, my friend and I here were having a small discussion. You see, we won a fuck ton of money just now, and the house gave us this bottle of vodka to get through, but I don't know if we'll manage it by ourselves, or what we could do afterwards. Can you help?'

I was cringing like fuck at that bit, but the girls giggled and muttered agreements to each other before sitting down. One had blonde hair and was in a baby blue dress. The other had raven hair and was in a black dress. Both had a lot of make-up on, slim waists, and large chests. I've never been a fan of that heavily made-up look, but when I look at Briscoe to say something he had this primal look in his eyes that tells me to stay quiet. Instead I follow his instructions to scoot over to the other end of the booth so that the girls could sit in the middle. Blue dress/blonde hair sat closest to Briscoe, while the girl with black hair was next to me.

'Ladies, do you have names?' Briscoe asks.

'Megan,' says the girl in the blue dress.

'Ashley,' says the black dress.

'Briscoe,' says my mate, taking their hands and doing that

weird limp fish handshake that if blokes do to one another is frowned upon, but seems to be the norm when greeting a woman. Megan and Ashley cooed a bit at each other. I kept my head down to look at my drink.

I wish I'd had a haircut and trimmed my nails before tonight.

'This is my good friend, Nick,' Briscoe says, directing the girls' attention towards me. They only smile at me, albeit sweetly, but nothing more.

'So, what are you guys up to tonight?' Megan says as she reaches out to pour herself a drink from our bottle.

'I'm on shore leave from the navy,' Briscoe says, 'haven't been back in the UK for quite a while, so I'm enjoying catching up with some old friends like Nick here.'

'The navy?' Ashley says. 'That's cool. Where was your boat?'

'I've been in Singapore the last few years. Real nice out there, real hot. But a good place to travel around from.'

'What kind of boat are you on?'

'I'm not on the boats,' says Briscoe, 'I'm logistics.'

Ashley's face dropped, but I've seen Briscoe do this bit a dozen times. He knows the girls think he'll be some high-ranking sailor, or maybe even a pilot, and saying logistics just isn't as sexy. He's got this bit down, though. I wish I had the gift of the gab like him.

'Let me tell you what being a sailor is in the twenty-first century; it's dead easy. All ships are now are giant floating computers. All sailors do is use a computer to sail a bigger computer out to somewhere so that their flying computers can go and do something. They won't even need pilots in a few years; ever hear of a drone? What I do is make sure that that ship has what it needs – repairs, supplies, personnel, equipment – to go out and do its job. Everything from bog roll to bullets gets on that boat through me.'

'I guess that is kind of impressive,' says Megan, her half joking pout turning into a sideways smile that puts a dimple in her left cheek.

'Kinda? You try keeping a navy ship running when it's half a world away from home port. But, it means I do have very, very good attention to detail,' he says, winking as he leans in and puts an arm around Megan.

'Are you navy too?' Ashley asks me. I'd just been spectating, the little dance Briscoe was doing alien to me, and it takes a while to realise that I've got to respond.

'Oh, uh, no. I'm not,' I say.

Ashley nods and keeps looking at me, but I've got nothing. The fuck am I supposed to say to her; no, I spend my days on my computer at my mum's house?

'He's in IT,' says Briscoe, jumping in and trying to make the save. 'Security. Gets paid big money by banks to try to break their security systems online. It's actually pretty cool.'

Total lie; I've got no idea how to do any of that stuff. But credit where it is due, he did make any job in IT sound a lot cooler than it actually is.

'So, you're, like, a hacker?' Ashley asks me, inching closer. I can smell her perfume and take in a big breath of it.

'I mean, not really. It's more like product testing. It's not what it sounds like.'

Ashley moves away again, and I shoot Briscoe another

look begging for help. He doesn't notice this time, as he's too busy helping Megan finish making her drink. Ashley slides over and taps her friend on the shoulder before both excuse themselves to use the restroom. Again as both go out of sight they shoot smiles back at Briscoe. He grins at them too, but when they're gone he swings his head back round towards me looking properly pissed off.

'What do you think you're doing, Nick? I set you up, she was actually a bit interested, and then you go and blow it?'

'But I'm not in IT, I don't know shit about what you were talking about.'

'Think that matters? They don't care, and you shouldn't either.'

'But I'm not that.'

'I don't keep ships running, the navy works nothing like that. And there's a hell of a lot more to being a sailor than floating computer systems around the globe. But, fuck man, they don't care about that.'

'Just doesn't seem right, you know? Pretending and stuff. They'd figure out what I am eventually.'

'Eventually? Christ, Nick, you're not looking to marry these girls or anything, and they sure as fuck aren't looking for that from you. Know what this is? This is us looking to get laid, and them being able to say, "Remember that time we were at the casino looking for high rollers and met that navy guy and his genius IT friend? We helped them blow through their winnings, they were hot, and we had fun." That's all this is.'

I get his point but Briscoe is laying it on strong. Wish he'd shut the fuck up. Feel small enough already.

'I know that the Quarry is a shithole,' he says, 'but when was the last time you even got laid, man?'

'I was talking to this one girl down at The Falcon a few weeks ago. Had a few drinks. She was nice, but—'

'Had drinks with? Fuck, I'm not talking about that. I'm talking about the last time you went out, took someone home, and fucked them?'

I look down at my drink instinctively before a smash of panic comes. I have to give him an answer, any answer, anything that would stop the inquisition and move him on. I'm fucking awkward with girls, alright? Why can't I just tell him to leave it. I feel like a fat enough pile of shit without him adding a sprinkling of shame on top of everything. I know I'm not normal; other people go out like they're on safari big game hunting, and I'm the one too scared to take part so sit back in the lodge.

By the time a sentence starts to come out of my mouth Briscoe has already clocked that it's going to be a lie.

'Fucksake, Nick. What have you been doing with yourself? Don't tell me you're turning into one of those sad fucks who sit at home on their computers all day.'

I try to give Briscoe something, to defend myself somehow, but from behind him I see the girls coming back. This time when they sit down they go either side of Briscoe, Megan back where she was and Ashley the other side of him, two bodies a distance away from me.

Briscoe sets about making Ashley a drink, and I look at the space between me and Megan; a metre-long void that segregates me away from the other three. I'm probably staring but they're not paying attention to me, and I just wish that I could try again and one of them would sit and talk to me. I'm looking along the bench until I see Megan's thigh, her dress rolled up and her not caring. I can't even remember any more what it'd be like to feel it and run my hand up its smoothness.

'Nicky, you alright, bud?' Briscoe says, and when I look up he's looking at me with a wrinkled look of concern. The girls are looking across him, giggling to one another, and I'm well aware that I am the joke.

'Fine, just fine. Not used to vodka drinks, just had a little too much is all. I'm going to smoke, get some air. Sorry,' I say, getting up and walking away from the table. When I'm at the edge of the bar area I want to look back through instinct, but the sound of another loud laugh from both girls tells me I shouldn't.

I walk through the casino floor and put my token into a machine at the lowest stake I can find until a waitress comes over to take a free drink order. As soon as it's there and I've drained it, I cash out before heading back outside to smoke.

It's one of those good winter nights, crisp and stinging deep in your nose when you breathe in. It's a strange sensation when mixed with the warm smells of foreign food coming from the late-night restaurants. I wander away from the front door of the casino to one of the benches. It's late now, but the human traffic is still heavy. I'm going to have to get the night bus home. Maybe I should get it now; I'll be nothing to Briscoe for the rest of the night. I light another cigarette and inhale deeply, trying hard to choke back the anger inside.

All I want to fucking do is get up and go, leave the casino and Briscoe and those girls and scuttle back to the Quarry, but I don't want to give them the satisfaction. I want to see this out to the bitter end, even if it means Briscoe doesn't get his dick wet tonight.

No, it's more than that. It's an ugly, angry jealousy and I don't know if it's at me or everyone else but it's telling me that I want to stay here and I want to find someone to fuck. To do what Briscoe was doing so successfully inside, to do what it seems like the whole world does so successfully. Maybe Briscoe is right; I should go back to the VIP section, sit up at the bar, and just lie my arse off to some poor little girl. Tell her that I'm in IT, or a banker, or an engineer, or a pilot, or anything, and how I'm having some down time between jobs and have got nothing except a big pile of cash and eyes for a girl to spend it on. Or no, not even that, I don't really care about that, it's something bigger; it's the meaning behind it.

What I had been too scared to say to Briscoe earlier is that I hadn't had sex since I left school twelve years ago. Since before Dad died. Since before the recession and the jobs went and I bloated up to twenty-something stones sat at my desk in my mum's council house, fucking about on my PC all day.

But it's not just sex, never just sex. I could get a few hundred quid off of Briscoe, find an escort and a hotel room, and get my fill. But that girl won't want to be there. You can have all the money in the world, all the success you want, but you can't buy validation. I'd still be lonely.

What I want more than anything is to lay down next to

a woman, go to sleep with one arm under her head and the other wrapped around her holding her breast, smelling her hair as I nuzzle against the back of her head. To have us both wake up in the morning, recovering from whatever positions we'd soundlessly moved into in the night and intertwine our bodies again, her head on my chest, until we're kissing, and she's on top of me and slides me back inside her. I want to be wanted and to be sought after and not to be a fat fucking sad sack.

I both fucking hate Briscoe and would give anything to be him and not feel like I was so utterly and irretrievably broken.

When I go to light another cigarette I realise my hands are shaking. They're no better when I head back inside. Before going back to the others I swing into a bathroom to splash water on my face.

I go up and back to the booth except there is no sign of Briscoe and the girls. The bottle of vodka is gone too, with just the empty ice bucket left. I look around a few tables but can't find any sign of them. Ask the barman if he'd seen them leave as well, but he couldn't help.

I check my phone and have a missed call and text, both from Briscoe.

> Hey man, we're moving the party. At the W hotel round the corner. Getting a room. Can't find you so head that way.

I could get on the night bus, go home and sleep this drink off. Perhaps I should. Or perhaps Briscoe will have put in a word. Smoothed over where I fucked up earlier. He's a good friend really, does nice things like pays for a night out when he knows I can't. Not a dick about it either; there's a big difference between sporting someone for a night, and making a sport of them. I should cut him some slack.

My phone tells me the hotel is just around the corner so I set off through the night. As I walk down I see a group of women sat at the bar, all have to be in their late forties or early fifties. They're dressed the same as Ashley and Megan were and are getting a round of drinks; glasses of white wine and shots of tequila. When the barman brings them their drinks he shoots them a grin, and as he goes to put their card through they all break out in the kind of cackle you thought only dirty old men and schoolgirls made. Is this what my mum does when she goes out with her friends these days?

Maybe they should know better, realise they're not teenagers any more and act their age.

Maybe they should realise that no amount of spin classes, make-up and body-shaping underwear will make them look like they did when they were twenty-five.

Maybe I should stop being a little bitch for denying that in their heads and hearts they still are twenty-five, and stop being bitter just because they were looking to get laid too.

I need some sleep. The hotel is real close, and I start off towards it, head down and looking at my phone for the map direction. As I'm walking I get another message through from Briscoe: Got the fucking suite. It's sick. Where are you

I reply that I'm coming, and he sends me the room number.

Great. Think I did some rescue work with Ashley ;)

The hotel is the same as the casino: glass, wood, leather, bright lights and sexy people. I move through the lobby as quick as I can, head down, until I get to the lift. I hit the floor for the room and it's one right at the top.

Briscoe's done some legwork with Ashley. Probably lied a bit but who cares, it's something. I'll take it even if she's just polite with it, doing her friend a favour by hanging out with me while Megan and Briscoe get up to something. After two stops I'm the last one left in the lift and I look in the glass. There is some positive shit here. In the lift mirror I fix my hair a bit. Might just be the drink but it doesn't look that bad. If I stand side-on then I can morph my body and, even if it's momentarily, it looks like I'm a little bit built. Like a shot putter or a prop or something. Not muscular, but powerful.

The lift dings and I snake through the hallway until I find the room. I knock but the door has been left ajar so it just pushes open. I say hello into the empty main room, and wonder if it's the right place until I notice signs that the other three have been here: Briscoe's boots, Megan's handbag, Ashley's heels.

The suite is fucking huge. You walk into a living room as big as the entire downstairs of my house, sofas around a table in the middle and a giant glass window looking out over London's skyline straight ahead. I close the door behind me and walk over to it. The whole West End is glowing.

There are four doors coming off the main room, all

closed. I should check to see where everyone is, rather than be lost in the fact I'm in a hotel room big enough to lose three people in.

From behind one of the doors I hear a laugh, squealing out for somebody to stop doing something in a way that screams that they absolutely, in no uncertain terms, do not want whatever it is to be stopped. Then another girl chimes in with a laugh, and I pick out Briscoe's low rumble as well.

I creep over to the door the sounds are coming out from behind, hand out ready to touch the knob, when I hear Briscoe's voice.

'I've seen some things, girls, but you two kissing with my cock in the middle tops the lot.'

I get gut punched with a swirl of anger and fear. He's in there with both of them, doing all the things I only wish I could be doing.

'One of you on my face, one on my dick, now,' I hear him say, followed by laughs. I can't tell the girls' voices apart but both are eager for the ride.

I don't move away from the door and stand planted, listening in to the cadences from inside; spikes of laughter descending into lower, more elongated moans that resonate through the door. I don't know if it is real or an act but the pair of them are moaning like the internet's best.

I have to back away. I look around for the bottle of vodka but they must have it in the room. For a moment I sit on the sofa but I hear one of the girls yell 'fuck' loudly, I jump up and storm out the room. I pant as the lift goes back down to the lobby, and have a cigarette lit as soon as I walk back into the quiet London streets.

I pace around outside of the hotel, and looking up I swear I can tell which room I was just in, looking down over everything. In my head I can definitely still hear the girls moan. I walk away until I find a bench to sit on. A couple are walking down the road, hand in hand, with her every now and then leaning her head on his chest. He is tall and broad and looks like a swimmer and she is small and Asian and they both look happy and I fucking hate them.

They see me, panting and swearing and smoking, and go to the other side of the street.

I hate this. I want more to drink. I want to get stoned. I want to sleep. I want to fling myself off of London fucking Bridge. It's more than frustration; I'm not one of those bitter blokes who go through life hating women for them not wanting to fuck me. At least, I don't think. But I need an outlet and what the fuck am I supposed to do about that? I can go back to the casino, drink the rest of that money, or buy a bottle of something and get hammered by myself back in the hotel room, or take a sad night bus back to sleep it all off at Mum's, but what's the point? Everything inside will still be there when I wake and sober up.

There's nothing to do because who speaks of these things? What kind of man sits down at a bar and complains that he hasn't had sex in a few years, but feels more lonely than frustrated because of it? Who admits that they aren't who they want to be, that they're hurting, and that all this is bearing down?

Nobody talks because nobody will listen because nobody will talk. It's all alien, so instead we bottle it up and shoot down anyone who will talk. Anyone who hears it tears down someone else's walls and uses the rubble to build theirs up a little higher because, yeah, they might be feeling the same, but at least they're not the weak ones; breaking down and crying out for validation and comfort like a fucking baby without a bottle.

My phone vibrates.

> Bruv where you at? Sorry if you walked into something mate

I ignore it. Briscoe calls, but I hit red.

> C'mon mate. Lets talk. I can explain.

I don't want to talk about it. Briscoe has already got so much over me, I'm not giving him this too. I stand up and start walking. I want to walk away, walk until dawn, walk until these stupid dress shoes have given me blisters and my ugly thighs are chafed red. To walk to the river, over it, just keep walking and walking until everything on the outside is shredded away just in case it lets everything bent up on the inside float away.

Briscoe calls. Red again. Text message.

> I'm worried mate. Just me here now. Girls are gone. Please call.

I don't walk away. Instead I go back towards the hotel. I'm not going to tell him anything, but if I can get one solid punch in it'll be all I need. I need to let him know somehow.

Even non-combat roles have to know how to handle themselves and I know he won't lamp me one back, but I need to get something in on him. He fucking deserves it.

I get back into the hotel, lobby now emptied out of its human decoration, and get in the lift. I only take a small peek at the mirror, but this time I only see a red-faced, wheezing person that I don't like the look of. When I get to the room the door is shut, and after hovering my hand in front of it for a little while I eventually knock. I hear quick footsteps, uneven through alcohol, rush towards it.

I clench my fist and put my lighter in my hand.

'Fucking hell, Nick, I was worried about you, mate,' Briscoe says, grabbing me in a hug and pulling me inside. He holds me in a big squeeze until I can't do a thing and drop the lighter on the floor. Maybe I am just a fucking coward.

'Took a walk is all,' I say. 'Needed to clear my head. Bit too much to drink.'

'Fuck that,' Briscoe says, 'let's have some more.'

I follow him over to the table in the middle. There are two tumblers and an ice bucket there, along with the now half-empty bottle of vodka. He refills his and makes me a new drink.

'Sorry if I was full-on tonight mate,' he says, looking out of the giant window across London.

'It was a fun night,' I say. Never been one for the late-night, drunken amateur dramatics which I know he's trying to start.

'No it wasn't, not for you,' he says.

'It was. I'd never have done this off my own back.'

'Fuck that, man. Fuck that. I was a dick to you.'

'Nah, you weren't, you took care of me.'

'My life is fucking shit, mate,' Briscoe says to the middle distance, 'real fucking awful. I'm always miles from home, made to feel the small man because I'm not on a ship when I'm out there. Half the people I work with aren't even navy. Most people on boats don't think I am either. At least, not like them. I'm just some sad fuck hanging on to their glory, you know?'

I say nothing. The drink goes down with the ease that being hammered brings.

'So I come back here and act like a big fucking deal. That I travel the world, but really I just go somewhere by myself to get away from fuckers who make me feel like shit. Like I hang out in far-flung bars picking up women, when if I want it I've got to pay for it. Paid those two tonight as well, you know? Anyway, then what do I do? Come home and act like one of them.'

'It's okay,' I say to him. Really, I've got no idea what to say. Never heard him talk like this before. Never heard anyone talk like this before.

'It's not. I've come back from a tough day at work, boss giving me shit, and kicked a dog, you know?'

I stop looking out over the skyline and look at him. He looks small; thin wrist holding the glass, weak jaw bubbling. He's crying.

'And you're not a dog,' he keeps going, 'you're a mate. The only one from back around here who messages me, who keeps in touch, who seems to fucking care. Probably the only real friend I've got. I didn't want to go back to the Quarry because I didn't want a homecoming with nobody there.'

I want to give him a hug. I should be so incredibly fucked off at what he's saying – poor Briscoe with his money and travels and life abroad he's not quite happy with – but know why I can't. This time it's me reaching an arm out towards him, grabbing his shoulder and leaving it there for a few seconds too long so that he knows.

We both look out, him seeing the city he thought he'd escaped from and me the one I'm trapped in. The sun has started to stain purple, and we both sit and watch it get lighter, the neon of the square fading away to the new dawn, refilling our glasses in silence, together.

Modernisation

I used to like being a postie. Last of the real community jobs, you know? Back in the days of bobbies-on-the-beat and butchers who always 'saved this real nice cut, just for you'. It meant something to people. I'd be sat in the pub after work and they'd come up and thank me for whatever it is I'd brought them that morning, good or bad. Never had to buy a pint the entire month of December.

You'd see the years go by on your route, watch how lives changed about; bring the wedding replies, the christening cards, school reports, right up to uni letters. People'd wait to see you at the top of the drive, or see you as they were doing the washing up and rush outside. Could tell straight off if it was good or bad news they were waiting on. And they'd tell you too. After all, you were the village postie. You were a community person like the GP or the vicar or the landlord. I was happy to hear the good news, and never in a hurry when people got the bad stuff neither.

I loved it, loved everything about it. Used to be important stuff I delivered: exam results, job offers, letters from sons in the army, postcards from Mum and Dad on holiday. Now it's different. I go out on my new routes, and it's all red-headed bills, pizza menus, and anonymous brown boxes from Amazon. I used to think it was the job that changed. I hated the word long before it came – 'modernisation' – but I've got seven years until the pension so what do I do? We get sold to a private company and I get no choice but to put up with them swapping out bikes for vans, closing local offices for big depots, changing your regular routes every other bloody week. What satisfaction do you get delivering to strangers? Besides, half the complaints we get these days are from delivering to the wrong house, or us just not being able to find a place. When you got one route, you know where everyone is and how to get their post to them. It's important, it is.

Don't want to sound like one of those types neither, but at the sorting office now, it's just Poles and Pakistanis. Nothing against them, lovely people, I'm sure, but it's not the same as having your mates back there.

So I did used to think it was the job that got modernised. For a long time I was on a nostalgia trip, missing the kinds of days when it'd be normal to have Mrs Ketterstone down at number thirty-eight pop out and give me a biscuit and a brew, ask me to keep a special eye out for a package her son sent her from Australia. Then I could stop by the sorting office for a whiskey and a fag to ask the boys for the favour. Community, you know?

Wasn't the job, though. Not the people either really. World just got smaller, a bit more convenient. That post from Oz isn't as urgent if you can call them whenever you want, see a picture of your grandkid on Facebook instantly, or – worst comes to worst – be on a plane there the same day. It is the same all over: local butcher forced out by the supermarket, morning paper turned into a phone app, cheaper to get a six-pint jug of milk on the weekly shop than have it dropped off, it happens.

I remember, when the estate was being built, my old man was one of the workers on it. The Quarry Lane estate; out of the rubble of west London after the war, somewhere for good people to get good, affordable housing near decent jobs down at the plant. All government backed, course. Lot of hope around there then. I lived there as a lad, and it was nice. Moved off it after school was done, but stayed local. Mum was there until Dad died too.

Hadn't thought about the place in years. Most of my routes took me around the greener bits of west London, old buildings filled with new money. Even as your routes got changed up more and more, the people were still nice; gave you a smile, and most even slipped you a tenner at the end of the year.

I won't lie, when I got my umpteenth new rotation, I was excited to see Quarry Lane on there. I was buzzing in the depot, excited for work for the first time in a while. Be good to see if anything'd changed, who's living in my old house and all that. There'd always been chatter about the old estate, gone downhill and such, but I'd never paid it much fuss; I grew up down at Quarry Lane, I knew what was really what. I knew the people. Probably had half the lads I went to the pub with when I was a kid still living there.

'You've got to be careful, David,' one of the other posties said to me down the local the afternoon before I picked up the first rotation back home, 'it isn't like it was round there.

Keep your head down around there. Trouble always seems to hit on that route.'

'I grew up round there, mate,' I tell him, sipping on me fourth down at The Rose and Crown, 'I understand it.'

'Being off doing those village routes has made you forget,' he says as he finishes his drink off, 'just be wary, alright. When something goes wrong on a route, it's always that one. Don't want it happening to you.'

'I'm going to Quarry Lane, not the bloody trenches,' I snap, 'besides, I'm not soft.'

'The Quarry isn't what it was, David. Seriously. Times change,' he says, walking off to get home to bed. I needed to as well, it's getting late. Already six-thirty and I've still got to cook me tea before an appointment with a three-in-the-morning alarm. I neck the pint, nod to the regulars, and head home. I trust the guy, don't get me wrong, but he's being a bit of a diva. I grew up there, I know it. It's a bit of excitement, and I haven't felt that about going to work in a few years. Modernisation be damned, I'm going home.

It's rolling on seven by the time I get to the Quarry Lane route. I'd been in the depot by five, packing up the bags and loading them and a cart into the van. One of the other posties had told me a good place to park up – 'safe' he called it, but to me it just looked convenient, right on the edge of the estate – and I get to work, setting the first sorted bag into the cart. You get a little map on new routes, but I didn't figure I'd need it. Times move on but buildings do a good job of staying where they are. It's one of those dingy mornings that make you wonder why you do it. Isn't anything new, though, been that way since day one; summertime you wonder why anyone would do anything else, then you get this after-Christmas spell where it's all the miserable weather and none of the thanks. Sun still isn't properly out – Scottish farmers get to work in the light, but who cares if all we get is darkness down here? – and what shine it manages is muffled out by low grey clouds. It's wet but isn't raining properly neither, just that constant spitting mist that makes the world look dreary, the drab colours dripping down from the sky and coating everything.

Start out on the houses round the edge of the estate. Not much has changed with these, but they always were the nicer ones, closest to the posh old houses round the corner. Detached, little front garden, bit of room out back for kids to play, lovely they were. Built a bit close together by modern standards, and the white-painted stone walls were looking a bit sad on a few of them, but they'd held up okay. Cars out front of them were pretty new, and the mail was much the same as on the old routes I'd been doing, all letters from banks and such. Few handwritten ones for one house, must have had a birthday or anniversary coming up. Something happy at least; could feel the badge through the envelope on a few and you hardly give them out for people heading to a wake.

I do both sides of the street, head back to the van, and load up a bag to go a bit further in. The way that Quarry Lane is built, the next few streets I do are much of the same. On the outside you have the detached houses, the ones that are a bit more expensive, then you get a few streets of terraced houses, and it's all maisonettes at the heart of it. I grew up in one of the terraced ones, and the lads from down my street would play footers against the ones from the maisonettes on the big rec ground at the heart of the place. Never played with the ones from the detached houses; they mostly went to different schools, think their parents told them to keep away from us. Never got why people would think that because I lived in a smaller house, had a dad who built things rather than sat at a desk, I'd be trouble. Class was a bigger thing then, I suppose.

I get a move on with the terraced streets, but save mine to last. Want to get ahead of myself so I can savour it a bit.

From the get-go I realise the terraces where I grew up have changed, all looks a bit alien. It sounds stupid, but it's the little front gardens that show it. When I grew up round here, everyone took pride in their garden, even if they were only as wide as your little house and barely two metres long. They made the street look nice, gave you something good to come home to. Nobody really had cars back then, paying for the house was enough, so all the dads took the buses to work each day. You'd see them, walking back from the stop, or more likely the local pub, pointing out what they've done with the lawn, bird table they built, that kind of thing. Few even got competitive, silly as it sounds now; the idea of working-class lads getting all uppity about their petunias, whose were best and all, but it happened.

Walking down there now, the gardens are gone. I go up the paths and where you'd have once found people's pride there's only concrete to park old cars. Street was narrow, never built for each house to have two or three cars parked up outside, but it hurts to see the gardens like this. I remember my mum and dad fussing over that lawn;

May bank holiday getting me out to help dig the beds and all to get it in shape for the start of the summer. Now each of them are uniform in having poured concrete, turned dark green from the moss and lichen with little puddles sitting where it's been done uneven and cheap. A few had the telltale dry footprint on them of where a car had been left overnight, but most looked like they hadn't moved yet that morning. Only greenery left is a few dying plant pots, whatever was once in them killed off by the winter's frost.

I rush with the first two bags for the terraces. Doesn't feel right. It's pretty quiet out, much less traffic than what I'm used to. A few cars drive by but I keep my head down, not too sure what to make of everything. I get to the last handful of letters from the second of the bags and as I'm walking up the drive I see a woman doing the washing up in the window. She looks about forty, might be a bit older, old black T-shirt with no sleeves on and her dark hair in a ponytail. Quite pretty, really. Her right arm has got intricate black tattoos from wrist to her shirt. Her top is pretty low-cut too, and it looks like the chain of patterns keeps going across to her chest. Not normally a look I like in women, but I bet when she's made up she can really pull it off.

Scrubbing away at a plate she looks out the window and catches my eye as I'm walking up to the letter box. I give her a big smile and a wave, same as I've always done when someone's seen me coming. She looks at me confused, perhaps a bit of anger in her eyes, but it's hard to tell. Don't want to be harsh but her front windows are pretty dirty.

It looks like she mouths 'what?' at me, and so I walk a bit closer to the window to give her another wave. Can see the emblem on my shirt then.

She watches me get close to the window, and starts to back away from the sink. I pause, no idea what's going on, and wave at her again.

'Fuck off,' I hear from through the window, and as she turns and scurries out of the room I can see she didn't have any bottoms on. She tries to cover her backside with her outstretched hand as she backs away, but it doesn't do much good; I can see she has a tattoo there as well.

I put the letters through the door in a hurry, don't want her coming out and making this more awkward. I hear her from inside, though, calling out to someone called Mark to come and sort it out, so I get a move on.

Never had something like that happen trying to say hello. Did she think I meant something by it? Don't see how she could. I'm the bloody postman, it'd be dodgy if we noticed each other as I wandered up the drive and I didn't at least give her a smile. I turn the corner to get off of the woman's street and I can see the van back where I left it. There are a couple of lads there, though, on tiptoes, peering in through the passenger window. They've got school uniforms on, but the cheap kind; all generic, supermarket stuff. Under their black coats I can see they've got blue jumpers on. Whatever happened to the school blazer? The kids haven't seen me coming, but they must've seen what they're after. Start pointing at something. Happens every now and again, couple of kids having a peek at what's in there, looking out for a package or something. Usually a video game, maybe a new gadget. Nothing unusual. I give a little puff of air out as I walk over to them and give myself a pep talk; just because you've had one little interaction end a little peculiar doesn't mean they'll all be that way today.

'Can I help you, boys?' I say as I get a bit closer, trying to sound cheery. Normally the lads will get down, look a bit sheepish like they've been caught doing something they shouldn't. Not these two; taller one keeps peering, shorter one looks at me.

'Anything good in there?' he asks.

'Probably, I've got all of the post in there. Someone will be getting something good. You two waiting for something?'

'Maybe we are. Let us have a look, then,' the lad asks me again. He can't be more than twelve but talks like he's much older.

'Can't do that, but where do you live? I'll let you know if I've done your street yet.'

'Why'd you want to know where we live?' the taller boy asks.

'So I know if I've done your street, or if it's still in the van.'

'That big box there,' the tall says, and I just know he's pointing at a huge Amazon package I've got in there, 'think that's what we're after.'

'Well, tell me what your address is, and I'll let you know if I'm going to drop it there.'

'Nah, that's the one. We'll have it now.'

'I can't do that, but like I say, let me know where you live and I'll let you know if I'll be dropping it off there. It'll be ready for when you're back from school.'

'Why you so eager to know where we live?' says the shorter boy.

'Nah,' says the tall boy before I can get a word in, 'I've heard about people like him on the news. I know what he is.'

'Yeah?' says the short one.

'Oh yeah. He's one of those paedos,' goes the tall one with a wicked smile.

'That right?' says his short mate. 'You some kind of fuckin' paedo or something?'

'What? No,' I say quick, the word thrown at me making me feel scared more than anything, 'just the postie. Trying to see if it's yours.'

'Alright, paedo,' the short one says back to me.

'Paedo postie,' the taller one joins in with a laugh.

'Stop that,' I say to them. I hate that word – vile, vicious word – and here they are flinging it at me on the street as a joke.

I don't like any of this and keep my eyes keen on the kids as I pick the cart up, put it in the back of the van. It's heavy and moving it so quick pulls at my old back, but I don't want to hang around. Truth be told, if they really wanted to, they could jump me. I keep myself against the van as I go around it to the driver's side, quickly unlocking and then re-locking the door. The empty post bags get thrown onto the passenger's seat and I floor it. Actually manage to get the clapped-out, speed-limited Transit to squeak as I drive off.

I look in the mirrors and back behind me the boys have stopped their nasty chant.

They seem to have lost complete interest, and I watch

them as they calmly and quietly pick up their bags and keep walking towards the school.

The getaway I make is a bit quick for the narrow streets, but there aren't many cars about. I stop when I see my old street and kill the engine, letting my hands shake on the wheel. Bit of me doesn't even want to go see the old house. This place has changed and I don't know if I can take seeing the garden that Mum and Dad fussed over be a parking space for a clapped-out old Fiesta, or the bedroom I grew up in now housing a lad who'll yell 'paedo' like it's a joke. Can't imagine seeing the living room where we had Christmas so many years, where we had Dad's wake, be lived in by someone who has seen so much nastiness they think the worst of a smile. I can imagine what the old living room looks like now; mismatched, threadbare sofas and a gaudy modern telly where Mum carefully arranged her figurines. Probably got the same wallpaper in there too, but now stained brown with smoke and sun-faded to dilapidation.

I've got to get it done. Been a postie pretty much all my life, through storms, snow, and heatwaves, and I've never skipped out on a route. The Quarry isn't taking that away from me too. I can be in and out of my old street quick. The maisonettes won't take long either, they've all got communal boxes for post. Just got to do this one last street, my street, then it's the final stretch.

I have to make myself get out of the van and unload the cart, override the fact that my body is screaming out to just drive away back home. I put the post bag into it and make my way down the road where I used to play football after school. I keep my head down, knowing my old house is down the far end and not wanting to look at it. Rather than do one side on the way down and one on the way back like I should, I zig-zag between the houses whose once white concrete-and-stone walls are now varying shades of moss-green and dirt-brown. Anything to put it off. I know I'm being stupid, that I'll get to it eventually, but that doesn't stop me. Each house I go to gets more painful, thinking of the people who built those houses, turned them into homes, after the War finally able to have something to call their own and make a life with. Now it's all cheap Ikea art where service medals once hung.

Perhaps it won't be like that, though. Some of the houses around here have held up well, been taken good care of. Mine might have fallen to a nice family, and it'll be sparkling white with a nice front garden. I'll wave to someone doing the dishes in the kitchen and they'll come out to collect the post. I'll tell them I used to live there, and they'll invite me in for a cuppa. We could have missed a box in the loft or something when we were clearing out and we'll sit down together and go through it. I'll show them my past and they can show me their present and the little house I grew up in can be a bastion against all of this.

When I've only my old house's letters left in my hand I walk up to the gate and see just how wrong I could be. The house is everything I didn't want to see. The garden's gone, now home to an old Corsa. The walls are green with moss, and dark brown stains run down from the gutters where they've long since been clogged with leaves and overflow. I can't see inside, and would swear the curtains keeping me out were the same ones as Mum had proper pride in, buying on a payment plan from a catalogue. I feel my throat get tight and try to choke me out, stop me from seeing any more of it; it's all I can do but keep from blubbing in the middle of the street.

'There you fuckin' are,' I hear from behind me, and as I turn I see two blokes striding towards me. Both look early forties, jeans-and-polo types. Armfuls of tattoos, and not well put-together ones like the lady I'd seen earlier. Cheap, with dull colours and thick, blurry lines.

'What is it you think you're doing?' one of them says now I've turned to face them. He's about my height but leaner, hair so short it's a clipper cut but he's gelled it anyway. They keep their distance but the way they stand makes me all uneasy.

'I'm sorry?' I stutter out. I take a step backwards through instinct, they take one forwards.

'What is it that you think you've been playing at all morning?' the same bloke asks. His mate behind him worries me more, though. He's a big lad, much taller than me, and fat, yeah, but with enough definition to his body I know he looks after himself enough to give me worries.

'I'm just the postman,' I say, holding out the bit of mail in my hand as proof like a fucking child. Little bit sad. Whole lot of afraid.

'Fuck off you are,' the talker spits, 'you're something else, you are.'

He starts to walk towards me, big mate in tow behind, and I back up again. I leave the cart and turn, so I'm now walking backwards down the street. Towards the van. It's a few dozen metres away, but surely this is just teasing; letting me think I could get back to it.

'See, I had a strange start to my morning,' he says, all three of us backing up the street as he talks, ''cause there I was, eating my cornflakes, when the wife comes in saying the postman's stood there against the window, grinning at her while she does the washing up in her night stuff.'

The mate behind him rolls his neck and I could swear I hear it crack. Van's still about twenty metres away.

As we back up we pass number fifty-five, where I once nearly had the daylights whipped out of me for taking the head off a rose when I was wrestling with a mate for the football.

'So I tell her she's got to be being silly, must have been mistaken, but when I step out front for a fag and a cuppa, I hear two kids chanting "paedo postie" round the corner.'

'They asked about some mail, I just wanted to know what street they lived on,' I say.

Fuck, I hate how pathetic I sound.

'Don't give a fuck,' the big, quiet one speaks up, 'one of them was my lad. You think it's okay to be asking him where he lives? It's bad enough worrying about people like you going after him at school or at the church. Now I've got to worry about you coming to my house and trying your shit?'

'I thought he was waiting on a package or something, I was just trying to help.'

'Nah, mate,' the front one says, 'but let us give you a hand, yeah? Don't know what kind of shit you're up to round here, but we ain't going to go for it. It's a proper community round here, we look out for each other, yeah? You think it's alright to stroll in here, perv at our wives, chat up our kids? No, mate, not even close.'

'I wasn't, I wouldn't. I mean, I grew up here, this is my community too,' I say, barely above a whisper.

'Like fuck you did,' the one at the back snarls. 'You're nothing like us.'

'Fuckin' save it, alright?' his mate follows up quickly. 'I don't want to hear your excuses. And I don't want to see you around here again, okay? Find some other place to go pester. Now go on, fuckin' go!'

They come at me, striding forward much quicker than before, and I drop the post for my old house. Walking the rounds keeps you in okay shape so I'm fitter than most my age, but I nearly stack it as I turn to run. Looking back over my shoulder I see the two, not chasing me but making sure I get on. The van is only ten metres away but it feels like it takes an age to get there, and when I do my nerves make me spill the keys onto the street.

'C'mon,' I hear shouted from behind me, and from closer than I expected, 'told you to fucking go, didn't I?'

It takes me a few tries to get the key in the ignition, enough time for the two blokes to be almost on the van's bonnet by the time it comes to life. I don't bother with the seatbelt, just grind the gear into reverse and get to going. I'm not delivering to the maisonettes, they can wait until tomorrow, or just not get their post ever again for all I care. I'll give the bags for here to somebody else, give the whole route to somebody else, give all of everything to everyone else – anyone else – just to be rid and gone.

When I drive by the post cart left abandoned outside of my old house I don't think to stop and pick it up.

I daren't drive back the way I came and instead head

out of the estate towards where the old high street was. It was a beautiful little run of shops when I was growing up, everything you'd need: paper shop, butcher's, greengrocer's, fishmonger's, barber's, hairdresser's. Most of the people who worked there lived around Quarry Lane too, or at least had done at some point.

The butcher's we used to get our Christmas turkeys from is now a Paddy Power bookies, open and ready for business as the clock hits ten. The greengrocer has turned into a Cash Converters, and the hairdresser's now sells kebabs. What was the barber's is now a corner shop, deals on cheap drinks written in marker pen on neon yellow and pink signs in the window. There is a new barber's further down, but its walls are covered in outdated, sun-bleached pictures of men with scissor cuts. In the window, they advertise special deals on all clipper jobs.

At the end of the street is the old pub, The Falcon. I had my first pint in there forty-odd years ago now, on a New Year's Eve. My whole family – well, seemed like the whole of the community – was down there. I'd had me first cheeky bottle of something down the rec ground, 'course, but when it was getting towards midnight I remember my dad handing me a pint of ale and winking. After I got it I locked eyes with the landlord – Reg, his name was, great fellow – and he smiled and shrugged at me. Nobody cared, it wasn't a big deal back then.

The pub hasn't changed. It's a big, dark red brick building with black wooden beams.

Old as well, one of those places which sprung up naturally on the roads out of London as inns. It has outlasted more wars and change than I could ever hope to see, and still looks good for it. The signs have been updated a bit, but still look like they did when I went there. Had a few licks of new black paint too, and the letters above the door are metal now, but it's still The Falcon.

While I'm stopped to examine the place, I see the door is open. There's a sandwich board outside too, advertising fried breakfast.

I need a drink. I need a fucking drink. The two blokes from earlier might come in, look like the kind to be in a pub at this time of the morning, but I don't care. The estate might have changed but from the looks of it The Falcon hasn't. Plus not even those knuckle-draggers would be dumb enough to kick off in their own local.

There is a tiny car park down the side of the pub, only big enough for nine or ten cars, and my van takes up two spots. I'll have a word with the landlord, see if they mind; not exactly like I'm blocking people out in the busy after-work hours.

When I walk in the state of the place punches me in the gut.

There's a bank of fruit machines either side of the front door, and I see a few more down the back. The board outside might have been advertising breakfast, but nobody inside was eating. Sat at the bar were a few old boys talking, and more were with their papers at tables. On one of the slot machines towards the back of the pub, a pack of young lads grouped around it as one played. To a man with pints. Could have been a Friday evening, except it was ten on a Monday morning.

It's more than that, though. On the tables there were cheap, wipe-clean plastic menus. Drinks promotions were on brightly coloured promotional prints, and rather than the weekly meat raffle they just advertised that on Tuesdays you could get a worryingly cheap steak and pint combo.

The pub which Reg looked after the entire time I lived here, part of a long line of people who'd kept The Falcon running since its opening a few hundred years back, was now a chain pub. Cheap shots, microwaved food, and a doorman after six.

I go up to the bar anyway. A drink is a drink and despite the fact I've got more streets to do elsewhere I'm done for the day.

'Hi, welcome to The Falcon,' a chirpy young girl says. She's got an inch of make-up on and her tits out to pull pints in the morning. 'What can I get for you?'

'Bell's,' I answer.

'Ice with that?'

'Can I get a small glass of water, on the side,' I say, not trusting her to not drown the thing.

'Would you like to double up for a pound?'

I look at her. It's the morning, and she's offering me to double up. I know that it isn't really the morning for me, I've been up six or seven hours and it's coming to the end of my work day, but still. Reg and his lad always knew the shift workers, and knew when they were coming in. He might pull a begrudging hair-of-the-dog for somebody off to work, but would make sure they anchored a touch. He wouldn't let the lads get into trouble by pouring them booze until after work, and even then he'd recommend they go home for tea first. Part of his licence, he used to say, duty of care just like a doctor. Although, of course, once he was happy they'd been home and had work taken care of, that was another matter. Now here was some young thing, no idea who I am, offering me a double for a quid.

'Sure,' I say.

She puts the drinks in front of me and when I pay her my change from a fiver includes two pound coins. I get the water level right in my drink and lean against the bar looking out. I'd hoped there'd be pictures of Reg and Mark behind the bar and I could talk about them, perhaps Mark's kids running the place. But no, the name might still be above the door but The Falcon was gone too.

'David?' I hear from across the pub. 'David, is that you?'

I turn and look at the voice. He looks a few years older than me, but the shape of his face rings a bell.

'Yes,' I say, proper cautious. Normally I'll talk to anyone and their donkey but after this morning I'm cautious.

'It's Tom, Tom Rodwell. I used to live down the street; number forty-two.'

He looks nothing like the kid I knew. He drifted away when he was sixteen, skinny as a beanpole. Good at high jump on sports day. Got a job at Heathrow so that was that.

'Bloody hell,' I say, shaking him by the hand, 'is it good to see you.'

'What are you doing here?'

'Just finished my round. Covering it this week.'

'Gordon Bennett,' he says, draining a good dose of his

morning ale, 'I haven't seen you since we were kids. How've you been?'

We talk about our lives. He married, still works at the airport. Still behind the scenes, but senior now. Bought his parents' place on the government scheme and still lives at forty-two. I told him I was divorced, grinding it out to pension age.

'This the first time you've been back in, what, how long?' he asks after buying me another drink.

'Since Dad. That was twenty-odd years ago. And that was the first time I'd been back in yonks, too.'

'Christ. Well, the old place hasn't changed; you haven't missed much.'

I shake my head at him. I don't want to be rude, but he's wrong. If you're in a place long enough maybe you don't see it, but I've seen it today.

'I don't know, mate,' I say to him, 'I don't know if I'm coming back around tomorrow.'

'What are you on about? It's the same as it ever was.'

I don't tell him about my day, but shake my head.

'Everything I've seen today, mate, it's just been angry and nasty. It's changed.'

'I don't know what bits you've seen,' he says, sitting up a bit, voice getting stern with flatness, 'but it's the same place that we grew up in. Same community. Same families, mostly. Nothing's really changed here.'

I want to tell him how wrong he is, but can't help thinking about how, when I grew up here, the lads in the big houses weren't allowed to play with us in the terraces, or how us in the terraces were told to stay away from the maisonettes. How both my dad and my old headmaster at school both lived down Quarry Lane, but drank at different pubs.

I look back out across the bar and don't know what I'm more afraid of; that I'm right, or he is.

Coffee

It's 4.17 a.m., and another three hours and forty-three minutes until the pub opens and I disappoint the pretty girl who pours the first pint of the day for me yet again.

I should have had another bottle around here somewhere, but the last few weeks on second shift has been tough – start at four, end at midnight – and I've been having a bit more than usual. Restocking got lost in the tumble of thoughts which rise and fall between the first drink and getting whatever passes for sleep.

Three hours and forty-three minutes, and I'm already anxious.

I'd wanted to switch off tonight. Have an extra day off between shifts, making it three in a row as I swap from second to the overnight. Wanted to spend tonight in oblivion, bit of a blowout, before tapering off to try to get through a fortnight of overnights; play a mindless video game, put on a film, have the bottle and glass out on my desk and slide away until my body can't stay asleep any more without a top-up.

I should quit but it isn't that easy. People think that the hard part about quitting drinking is the mental side; how do you keep saying no in a world where alcohol is the commodity of friendship.

It isn't.

There's too much sunshine to get through between now and when the local Wetherspoon's opens for 'breakfast'.

Until I get to see Jane's sad smile.

I'll find a way to get through the next few hours. Three hours, thirty-nine minutes.

I'd quit if I had something to quit for that was bigger than the fear. I'm barely thirty but everything hurts these days: my heart pounds, I'm dizzy most of the time, and can sweat through two shirts during cold winter shifts in the warehouse. I feel like I'm waiting for the stroke, or the heart attack, or to collapse cancer-ridden, or to have oesophageal varices burst and drown from whiskey-swollen veins flooding my lungs, or bleed out as my guts fill with the red stuff.

But at least then I wouldn't have to live through the DTs. Most people think that 'DT' stands for detox. It doesn't. Delirium tremens.

After a few days of already feeling like hell – when the vomiting, sweating, shaking, and shitting yourself has died down – they kick in.

They're what kill you.

Believe it or not, I don't want to die.

I get out of my computer chair and go to the bathroom. The estate has quietened down, music from the downstairs neighbours has finished and next door have wrapped up their nightly fight-then-fuck cycle. I'm in one of the little studios at the top of the sprawling block of maisonettes in the heart of the Quarry. It used to be I'd stay up late to get to sleep in peace and quiet, bedtime somewhere between when neighbours go to sleep and the birds wake up. I had to do something to fill the time.

At least that's what I tell myself; why I'm still drinking at dawn after taking the shifts at times that most people don't want.

I have a cold shower, starting the water off lukewarm and then gradually easing off the temperature until I'm shivering. It's easier to lay shaking under the covers if you're cold rather than burning up.

I can't believe that I drank my back-up. Again.

The supermarkets here are barred from selling booze past eleven. The pubs shut at midnight. I'd even consider going to the club for a drink, if it wasn't for the fact it was a Tuesday and they weren't open. I don't even have any mouthwash left from the last time this happened. Don't have a car to drive somewhere out of town, and refuse to be the shaking fuck-up on the night bus.

I go through the kitchen cupboards again. You know how you sometimes stick twenty quid in your wallet someplace you wouldn't normally put money so you don't spend it, an emergency taxi fund on a sloppy night out, then forget about it? I do that with booze. Found a bottle of decent brandy I'd hidden in the bathroom cupboard behind the Toilet Duck once.

No such luck this time.

I put a *Lord of the Rings* film on – it's about as long as I'll have to wait until I can see Jane – and crawl under the covers.

By the end of the first act I need to have another shower. I don't wash, and instead dry heave beneath the sound of the running water. In the end I sit down in the shower beneath the stream of water, concentrating on breathing in and out and spitting out little strands of bile.

When dawn finally brings its lazy arse around I quit on the poor attempt at sleep I've been trying. I shower again but don't wash my hair; if I did I'd lose balance, falling over and smacking my head somewhere. Vision has gone to shit and I feel wobbly. When I'm done showering I sit down to get dressed.

The pub is halfway between my flat and work. If I'm starting at 4 p.m. then I'll go there before. If I'm finishing at 8 a.m. I'll go there after. On days like this I'll go and lie about the situation being one of the other two.

Delirium tremens starts when this stops and is worse.

The bus is full of commuters and school children and I'm lucky to find a seat.

Probably a bit brutal rushing on and sitting myself down, should have looked around to see if someone else needed it, but with the stop-starting and turning, I'm sure I'd stack it. Instead I lean my head against the coolness of the window and turn my music up: *Monday at the Hug & Pint* by Arab Strap. I take the bus every day and know its turns and stops, but I open my eyes every few minutes to check the landmarks and make sure I haven't stayed on too long. *But sometimes when I'm with him, I just stop being me,* sings Aidan Moffat as I step off the bus. It's turning out to be one of those bright, low sun winter mornings and the harsh light makes my brain rattle.

The pub is only a few minutes away from the bus stop, but I stop by the corner shop which sells booze this early in the morning. Normally I'll pick something up from there on the way home, or to put in my bag as maintenance if I start to feel like this during a shift.

Today I pick up one of the pre-made gin and tonics to take the edge off and a paper to look at in the pub.

I don't know what's sadder: the fact I want to do this, that I need to do this, or that I'm doing it so I don't seem too strung-out for a barmaid who'll pour me a pint with sad eyes at eight in the morning.

Delirium tremens begins when this ends. Quitting isn't like in the movies.

No, what is sadder is that, after necking it on the street outside to stop my hands shaking, I didn't care that I'd had to.

I walk into The Sun and Moon a few minutes past eight and the place is empty.

Despite the lights being on, the whole thing looks a distinct shade of brown, from the faded faux-leather chairs to the hide-the-stains carpet and dark woodwork.

Jane isn't behind the bar. She always opens – I've joked about it with her before, she says she's always busy in the evenings so works the early – but it's just two blokes down the far end, chatting as they fill the fridges behind the bar.

What is saddest is that this part of my morning made me the most upset.

I hang around at the door, unseen. I should just go home again, pick up a bottle from somewhere. Could be asleep properly by ten or eleven for a few hours. See where the day goes from there.

Jane walks out of the back room carrying a tray of glasses. She's good to me, friendliest chat I get most days, but yeah, got to admit, she's fucking gorgeous. Deep dark skin, though still light enough so that you can see the shading on her tattoos. Short hair, shaved at the sides and a mohawk thing on top, all dyed electric blonde. Tunnels. Nose ring. Big smile, showing off perfect teeth.

To most people she'd be a manic pixie pop punk princess. I just like how she looks pouring me a morning drink.

I jog up the stairs to her end of the bar.

'Y'alright?' I say, putting the paper on the freshly wiped-down bar top.

'Heya, Coll, how are you doing?' she asks, scratching where the base of her mohawk meets her neck. She's started doing this since she got rid of her braid extensions a few months ago.

'Not a bad morning, how about yourself?'

She smiles. She's done her make-up well enough, but nothing can hide the trenches underneath her eyes.

'I need to sleep. Morning after morning is brutal.'

'Mornings tend to be,' I say, then feel like a class-A wanker for it. The most emo line ever.

'Anyway,' she says, 'what are you having?'

I want a whiskey. The gin on the way might have taken the edge off but I don't feel right. Not quite chucking-up-bile off again – yet – but still far from okay. It's that spacey feeling; like you're a passenger in your own head, disconnected from reality, watching the world's shittiest TV show.

'Carlsberg,' I say, thumbing two pound coins and a fifty pence piece out of my pocket.

'Coffee is more traditional in the morning,' she says to me with a huff.

She flashes me those eyes. Dark make-up around them accents the whiteness in them.

She's not being too serious, but it isn't entirely a joke either. Truth in jest.

Jane's young. I'm technically still young, but feel old. She's properly young. Maybe uni, maybe not, but definitely just out of school. Young enough that she's only used to seeing the people sat in pubs pissing their lives away being old men, either in little groups or, worse, spat out by life and alone. I don't fit that mould. I'm sure it upsets her.

Perhaps I'm overthinking this. She pulls pints for minimum wage.

'I keep telling ya,' I say after the first sip, 'it's not morning. Not in my world. I'm just clocking off.'

Jane slides eleven p change across the counter. I have a large change jar of ten p and penny coins from her which I'll take to the sorter down at Sainsbury's every few weeks. Usually enough for a few beers. One morning she gave me a five p and three two ps. I don't know why I remember that but it makes me smile.

My smile goes as I watch Jane's eyes change. She shakes her head a little, eyes getting small as she balls up her mouth, ready to spit something out.

'That's bullshit. That's an excuse, not a reason,' she says, a hint of Jamaican accent coming through her West London standard. I'd only heard it a few times, usually when telling blokes who got a bit frisky to get out. 'You can keep vaguely normal hours if you've got a reason to. There's always a way to stay connected to the real world if you want to, no matter how hard you find it.'

I tilt my head at her, eyes and brows scrunched into a confused pile. This isn't like her, not one bit. We joke, we laugh, we banter. She's pissed off. I'm sure there is something more than me going on here.

She's not wrong, though.

Jane breaks away and storms down the bar towards the back room. Behind where she was standing the fridges are nearly bare. Late-shift last night must not've bothered to re-stock. That'd put me in a mood too, or at least tip me over the edge.

With Jane gone I get along with the paper, flicking past the page with an especially fucked-up-looking Gaza on it. Like people with cancer, or anything which rots their bodies away, I tell myself I'd get rid of myself before I get into that state. At least I used to.

'Another?' Jane asks, curt and flat. I hadn't realised I'd drained the first one in a few minutes. When I look up at her, the whites of her eyes are stained slightly red.

'As you offered,' I say, trying to be charming. If I'm normal to her, she'll hopefully twig that I didn't take anything she said to heart.

She brings it back and I start digging through my pocket for coins. 'Don't worry, it's on me,' she says. Still flat, and I cock my head at her.

'You sure?'

'Yeah.'

'You don't need to, you know.'

'I was a bitch. Shouldn't have gone off on you.'

'Don't worry about it, seriously,' I say to her.

'No. I had a bad morning is all. You're nice, but I don't really know you like that to say those kinds of things, you know?'

'It's okay. I didn't take it to heart. And I appreciate this,' I say, holding up my glass. She mimes holding up an imaginary one, and we give a fake air clink. She smiles, warm like she usually does.

'Good. And don't read into it; I get bought a load throughout the day. This is just one of many in the bin.'

She smirked her normal smile at me, drama over. Jane said I was nice.

I'm not one of those sad, lonely fucks who sit around falling in love with any girl who is even remotely nice to them. That said, I want to fuck her, of course. To spend nights in bed, cigarettes and shots of whiskey and no clothes and punk rock and all of that clichéd fuckery. To rage at the good morning together, all of that shit. To only get a few hours' sleep and sit together on the bus from my flat as we go to our various jobs, making plans for me to meet her at the pub when I clock off and for us to do it all over again. We'd say we'll go gentler the next time, on our own bodies and each other, but then the drinks would pour and we'd rip each other's clothes off as we descend again.

I want to be the reason she has bags under her eyes.

Cigarette. That thought sounds good. I put a beer coaster over my glass – used to put the fag packet over it, until it had been nicked for the third or fourth time – and step outside. As I get towards the door I hear the two blokes down the other end of the bar laugh. Through instinct I look back over my shoulder and they quickly look away from me.

Wankers. Even though I'm the one with the better job and one of them is fat and ugly as fuck, they think they can have a laugh at someone in their pub in the morning. They couldn't handle proper shift work if their lives depended on it.

I smoke and come back in and there's nobody new apart from me, Jane, and the wank brigade. I order another beer. Should slow down. Maybe I should head home, can always tell when I'm going to get a bit silly due to how easy the first ones go down, but I know well enough why I'm not going anywhere. I pull a pen out of my satchel and start doing the crossword. It's a good measure, when a red top puzzle gets too hard I've probably had enough.

Jane comes back and absent-mindedly fills the fridges. I buy another beer off her, but she's quiet now, going about things mechanically. I think that perhaps when she's done with the shitty job of re-stocking she'll loosen up again, get chatty with me like usual, but instead she tinkers around.

'Did it occur to you,' I say to Jane when she's got her back to me, doing something or other behind the bar, 'that maybe I just enjoy shift work? That there's something fun in being on a different routine to everyone else?'

'You really want to do this?' she says to me, turning away from cutting limes.

'Don't have much else to do.'

'I mean, I suppose you could,' she says, 'still means you're not anchored to anything, though.'

I can see I'm not winning this one.

'How about you, then? Who voluntarily opens up a pub at the crack of dawn each and every day?'

She takes a step back. I've hit a nerve. We both scramble for words, her to try to find something to say and me to tell her she doesn't have to.

'Not here,' she says, stopping both of us, hand on hip and fluffing her peroxide curly hair. There's a flash of something across her face, scrunched eyes and a stuck-out jaw.

'Sorry, I—'

'It's fine,' she says, cutting me off.

'No, it's the same thing you did with me. We wind up spending so much time together, get a bit familiar.'

'It's okay, it's not that. I'd tell you.' She smiles, forced but sweetly. 'Just not here.'

Before I let my brain tell me that what I'm about to do is a fucking terrible idea and I'm about to get made a fool of and run out of one of the few places I feel both welcome and am able to drink in peace, I tear off a corner of the newspaper and write my number on it.

'I'd love to hear it sometime.'

Jane holds it in her hand, running it between her fingers. I see her trying to figure out if this is a good idea before reaching a hand around back and slipping it into her jeans back pocket. I drain my pint and put my paper in the satchel.

'Right, onwards and upwards, day waits for no man, carpe diem, and all that miscellaneous bullshit.'

'You go do your miscellaneous bullshit,' Jane says.

'I will,' I say loudly, then 'text me,' quieter.

She nods. I'm not done drinking, but leaving now has two distinct advantages: I can look a bit mysterious, and it nixes any chance I have of drinking too much before 10 a.m. and putting her off. When I walk out this time the wanker brigade is silent. Least in my mind they are.

I buy a bottle of Jack from the corner shop on the way back to the bus. It's overpriced but the supermarkets aren't selling yet and fuck waiting around.

I wake up with a cracking headache. Mouth is that special kind of whiskey-cigarette-vomit putrid. Half of the bottle of Jack is gone, sat next to a pile of crunched-up Coke cans. No wonder I feel like shit. This isn't taking the edge off, it's getting fucked up on a Monday lunchtime.

I'll have to pop out to try and get some more to get through the night. What time is it?

Track down my phone and it's a bit past seven. There's a text from Jane.

> Hey Coll, it's Jane from the pub. Are you around later x

The room might be spinning but I'm able to get my vision to centre by focusing on the little 'x' in her text.

The message had come through around four. Probably for the best I was passed out then, in case I'd have tried to reply. It's when I save her number as 'Jane Pub' that I realise that, despite my weird little fantasies, I don't know her surname.

Hiya! Sorry for not getting back to you, was having a little sleep. I'm not up to much. What are you thinking?

Message takes forever to write. Half through nerves, half through focusing on the screen giving me vertigo. Don't put an 'x' on the end; find it fucking cringeworthy when blokes do that messaging girls.

I roll out of bed towards the shower. On the back of the toilet there is a splatter of vomit that the flush couldn't reach. No idea when I did it but it seemed new.

I go through my routine: shower, teeth brush, vitamins, milk thistle, neck two pints of water. I should really eat something – it's drinking on an empty stomach that really fucks with your liver – but there's nothing in the house. I'll get some dinner when I go out.

When I get the balls to check my phone there's a reply.

Want to meet for a drink or sumthing x

Yes. Yes, I do.

We do a bit of messaging to figure out a when and a where. The Grange is about equal distance, fifteen-minute walk for me and fifteen on a bus for her, and we say nine.

Before I get dressed I clean my flat as best I can: vomit off toilet, empty bottles and cans bagged up, and at least trying to declutter. You get used to your own mess. Can't remember the last time somebody came over.

Not that I expect her to, but you know?

I only have one half-shot of Jack, just to ease things.

Same theory as a heavy coffee drinker needing an espresso to top up and cut off a caffeine headache.

Exact same thing.

I should taper off. In theory it gets you out of the danger zone without DTs. Just takes an age. And it's no guarantee.

Put on a casual shirt and jeans and head out the door. Smoke a cigarette on the way.

No idea if Jane smokes so just have the one, don't want her put off by smelling like an ashtray. The walk helps clear my head and I'm feeling good again when I get to the pub. I look around but don't see her.

I'm here

Sorry! Not used to buses at this time! Be about 15 x

That's cool. What are you drinking?

Jack and Coke x

You know what I said about not falling in love over small details? Fuck that. I could well be. I order myself a beer and figure I'll get Jane hers when I get my second or third. I stand at the bar and look around, sipping on a Peroni; the bar is quiet. It's packed after the office day kicks out, but then people filter away. There are a few eating dinner, most watching a football match silently; no commentary on, lest the softly sung, bullshit dinner party music be interrupted.

I order another pint and get Jane's drink too. I'm feeling

good to go again now, fresh beers covering up the damage last night's – well, this afternoon's – whiskey did. I'm over halfway through it by the time that Jane walks in.

Fucking Jesus wept I could be in love.

Red heels. Tight black skinny jeans. White top and short black leather jacket. Eyes and lips made darker than her skin through make-up. She's skinnier than her work clothes always made her look.

Play it cool, Coll.

I wave to her and drain my pint as she saunters across the room, leaving a trail of turned heads and sideways glances in her wake. When she arrives next to me neither of us really know how to great each other. We settle on an awkward side hug before she asks if that is her drink waiting.

Her eyes are still circled by the deep lines of exhaustion.

I tell her I ordered them when I got here, and tell her sorry for having it be sat so long. She either doesn't notice, or chooses not to comment on the fact that the ice isn't melted.

'Can we sit outside?' Jane asks. 'They've got those heat lamps here and stuff. Shouldn't be too cold.'

'Sure,' I say, and she heads outside to be the advanced party. When my beer arrives, I ask for a whiskey too and neck it.

It's been a while since I've been in a situation like this.

I sip the head off of my beer so I can carry it without spilling, but make a conscious effort not to drink. I might have bounced back from the brink, but these drinks are going down too easy again. This is why I don't like drinking with other people: there's this anxious panic about it. Will

I get enough? What if I drink too fast? I've got that half bottle of Jack but this could be a long night; no chance for sleep if I only woke up at seven. I'll have to pace it.

You'd think that a thought process like that would ring alarm bells. I would have thought that if you'd have told it to me years ago. You would, however, be wrong; it's amazing how quickly fucked up can become the new normal.

I go outside and see Jane under the red glow of the heat lamps. There are a few people stood up smoking out there, but we're the only ones with our drinks out at a table. I watch her stub out a cigarette before drawing out another long Superking from the pack and lighting it. She exhales the first drag with her head back, straight up into the air. The red glow of the lamps makes the smoke seem thicker than it is, and the way she looks she could be anywhere in the world right now.

I sit and she smiles at me. While she talks I light up a cigarette.

'I'm sorry again about earlier,' she says, straight off the bat, 'it wasn't an okay thing to say.'

'It's okay, really.'

'It doesn't matter if you're okay with it, though, does it? I don't feel good saying that to someone. You shouldn't say shit like that to someone.'

'I accept your apology,' I say to her. She smiles to herself, looking down into her lap, and takes a small sip of her drink.

'So what do you do,' she says, still looking at her lap before moving up to meet my eyes, 'that brings you in at such odd times of day?'

'Very boring things. I'm at the big JL's warehouse. The technical name for it is "compliance", but really it's snooping on people: inventory, watching cameras, spot checks. Pays a lot better than being one of the people you're snooping on, but doesn't exactly make you the most favourite person to go get a pint with.'

She nods.

'They shake up the shifts quite a lot,' I say, 'stop us getting in cahoots with people working there, I guess. But on the plus side, it means I see you most days.'

She nods again and looks down. It's hard to tell with the angle and the light but I think she looks happy.

On the downside, I'm relatively sure I slurred saying that. There's the old adage: if you think you're slurring a little bit you're slurring a lot, and if you think you're slurring a lot you're not speaking English.

'Do you like it?' she asks. I refocus.

'It keeps me in beer money. So I suppose it serves its purpose.'

The red glow goes out and Jane leans back to push the switch. When it comes back on I can see she has her belly button pierced, a dreamcatcher with gold strands running downwards.

'How about you?' I ask. 'Why do you open up a pub every day?'. I light a cigarette to smoke while I listen.

'Because it's the shift nobody wants, so they're always easy to get.'

'Then why do you want it?' I say deliberately.

'How long have you got?' she says with a laugh, finally drinking a proper amount of her drink.

I'm enjoying this but goddamn does she drink slow. Don't want to hurry her, or look like a lush by going up and getting another drink while she's still working on hers, but . . .

'I've got the time,' I say to her and smile.

'I had to move home last summer from uni. That bedroom tax shit. Mum has MS, bad, and my old room we used for the carer that would come for respite, during a flare up, whatever. But now it's too expensive to have a spare room, so somebody has to move back into it. And moving back into it means looking after Mum. 'Course my golden child brother doesn't have to think about it, so until we figure something out it's me.'

She stares off into the middle distance. I can see her eyes watery in the red mist.

It's the first time I've realised how far apart in age we actually are; in my head we were the same age. Perhaps her life has meant she's grown up and mine means I haven't.

'I'm sorry,' I say.

'It gets tiring. Especially when Mum's bad, like she is at the minute. I tried getting a regular job when I moved back, that good old nine-to-five thing, but you can't do that and be a carer. At least at the pub, nobody wants the morning shifts so I can be back by early afternoon to take care of her.'

'What were you studying?'

'Art history,' she says, snorting to herself. She wipes her eyes, which somehow don't wind up with the panda look. 'Yeah, I know, it's a nothing degree but it's fun.'

'It's not a nothing if you like it. Think you'll go back?'

'Oh, definitely, yeah. Figured I'd give it a year to work something out with Mum.'

We sit and we talk and we smoke. I match her drinking pace and don't feel too anxious. She tries to buy the next round but I don't let her, half through her story and half because it means I can have a cheeky extra drink at the bar.

Eventually I'm aware I'm drunk but after three Jack and Cokes so is she, or so she says, and we walk out rather than order another. I don't invite her back to mine and she doesn't ask to come but we are walking and talking – her about art, me about anything interesting I can blag – and wind up there.

When we walk in she takes her jacket off but leaves her heels on. The white top doesn't have arms and I can see both of her sleeves for the first time. Can't make her tats out properly, but she has both upper arms covered, along with her left forearm.

'Drink?' I ask her as she starts to look around my studio flat.

'What've you got?'

'Water, OJ, Jack, not a whole lot else,' I say.

'Any mixer?'

'I don't think so, sorry,' I say, head in the fridge. Running out of Coke and drinking it neat would explain the vomit earlier.

'Ice?'

'That I can do.'

'Then neat is good,' she says.

I put the bottle on the kitchen counter and search for

clean glasses. The only ones I have not dirty and vaguely matching are wine glasses, so I fill them with ice. I pour mine the same size as hers, and hers wasn't a big one.

I should taper from tomorrow.

I've heard benzos help with the delirium.

Tomorrow.

She is looking at some of the shit artwork I've got on my walls. It's all either Ikea junk or video game posters. While her back is turned I drain half of my Jack and quickly refill it to a little more than hers.

'Probably not up to your usual standard,' I say, handing her a glass.

'Whatever people put up is interesting,' she says, taking a tentative sip from her glass and leaving a dark black lipstick stain on the rim.

'Very bohemian,' she says, smiling and holding up her wine glass of whiskey. I smile.

Drinking whiskey out of a wine glass with an art history girl. So fucking hipster cliché.

I'm still smiling, I realise.

I've got a small sofa and we sit and we're talking. If she finishes her degree she might learn how to tattoo. All of hers are classical, and she tells me which paintings inspired which ones and I do my best to listen and pay attention but after the cold air of the walk home the drink is really hitting me hard.

I put my glass down. I could well balls this one up. Benzos help.

She is showing me a tattoo on her right arm, me sat to her left, explaining what a line of Latin means, twisting her body to invite me to follow its path as it winds around her body. As I lean across her our faces get close, and I'm fucked up, yeah, but I know that moment before a kiss, when you're in each other's personal space, mouths close, and we lock eyes before we both lean in and do it.

I am kissing Jane.

She has the softest mouth I have ever kissed.

I stop leaning over her and sit back down, and she swings her body over towards mine. As I settle the world spins a little bit and my stomach sends a wave of something unpleasant but I ignore it as she throws her leg over to straddle me.

As we kiss she takes her white top off and she has a chest piece of a heart, wings of geometry snaking up to her shoulders to become the tops of her two shoulder pieces. I tell her it's beautiful and she smiles and says she wants wings on her back, same style.

We keep kissing and I run my hands along her hips and she unbuttons my shirt to put her hands on my chest. She is rocking and grinding and this should be the greatest fucking moment of my life.

I cannot get hard.

I do my best to keep my body in autopilot and tell my dick that this is it, that moment that you've thought of having sad and lonely wanks in your office chair, but nothing.

I unhook her bra and she doesn't stop me. She still has heels on and it should drive me wild.

She runs a hand down from my chest and unbuttons my jeans but there is nothing there for her to find. Fucking drink.

'Give me a minute,' I murmur to her.

She gives an anxious smile and I try to make this worth her while. I kiss down the length of one of the arms of her chest tattoo until I reach her breast, taking the nipple into my mouth and holding it between my teeth as I flick my tongue across it.

'Ouch, gentler,' she says. I mumble a sorry.

I try something different and try to pick her up to lay her down on her back, wrapping an arm around her little frame and hoisting myself up. As I try to stand, though, the world goes shaky and I nearly trip forward. She notices I'm off balance before me, and lets out a little scream, jolting her body back towards the sofa. We collapse, me sat back on the sofa and her half fallen off of me towards the side she was once sat.

She sits up with an arm covering her breasts. I don't feel good. Really, really, not good.

I mutter a sorry and sorry again before standing myself up, using the arm and back of the sofa to steady myself, before making a dash for the bathroom.

The first few heaves come out silently and, yeah, this is embarrassing, but it'll sober me up and I can get back at it. Brush my teeth and I'll be good to go.

Sometime around the time I start coughing up bile, tears in my eyes, I realise I haven't eaten today but have had umpteen drinks.

Shit. That's the thing that gets you fucked up and ruins your liver.

I slump to the ground when I'm pretty sure that nothing else is coming out in this round. Every instinct says to pass out then and there, heavy eyes and a head so bad it feels like it's going to sink through the floor. I'm drenched in sweat, and my legs ache from kneeling over the bowl.

Jane is there. I can't.

I splash water on my face and brush my teeth. Eyes are still red, though. Whatever, it's dark. You shut your eyes to kiss anyway.

'Sorry about that,' I say, walking back into the living room, 'don't know what's up with me tonight.'

There is no response. Jane isn't on the sofa. Her coat is off the rack by the front door. Of course. Why should I even be surprised?

Coll, you fucking idiot.

I look at my phone and nothing.

For fucksake.

My stomach is still raw but I pick up the whiskey with mostly melted ice and pour both drinks into one glass. I take a long hard drink of it and my stomach protests, but I'm able to keep it down.

When I light a cigarette, though, it pulls a hard acid reflux up from my gut and I feel it burning its way out.

I cough and have to run to the bathroom to deposit more bright yellow bile. This time I listen to my instincts and stay on the floor.

I don't know what hurts the most when I wake up. My mouth is that special kind of putrid. Again.

My brain has that special kind of splitting headache, where every movement sends a new jolt.

My back and neck are locked in a twisted S-shape from where I collapsed backwards when I was done chucking up.

What hurts the most is the immediate memory I have of last night. Of Jane being here and then not.

My phone still has some battery left but no messages.

Did you make it back okay last night?

I have to squint to type. The lock screen says it's not quite eight in the morning. At least I woke up at a normal time.

My phone vibrates.

Yeah

I stare at it for a while, and then close my eyes to let the single word, no 'x', resonate.

It's too much. I turn the shower on and slide my jeans and shirt off before sitting down under the stream of water.

Fuck it all.

My phone vibrates again. I pull my torso out of the shower and pick the phone up from the closed toilet lid.

Are you doing okay?

Yeah. Sorry about how it ended last night.

It's okay

I feel like shit but need to go out. Only got a bit of Jack left, but after what it's done to me in the last few days fuck that noise. I need something new. Not back into work until tomorrow morning, I need to taper it back off today. Get off this fucking bender. Could get the bus to Jane, bit of a hangover cure, then go shopping on the way home.

Are you working? I ask her.

It takes a long time for a reply to arrive, me still sat in the shower hoping that my body will just absorb whatever it needs from the stream of nearly-too-cold water.

> I don't think you should come in

Fucksake. I know I was drunk and it was a weird night and I saw her topless but I didn't fuck it up that bad.

How comes? Followed by It'd be good to have a quick talk about last night

I just need to explain, is all. I do shift work, so my daily habits are a bit off normal times. I got mixed up and didn't eat last night is all. That isn't like me. I was nervous.

She's the kind of girl you get nervous about. I just need to explain.

> You know what I've got going on. I can't add anything else to it.

Fuck her, then. Fuck her. Yeah, she's got a bad lot in life at the minute, but who doesn't? We're all just bouncing around trying to pay rent and make bills. Why does she get a free pass?

My heart is racing. My chest is tight. I turn the water colder.

Is my arm tingling?

Fuck her.

No.

The world will always kick back a lot fucking harder than you can kick it.

This is your fault, Coll. Jane wasn't the one to get too drunk to make out. To skip meals and get hammered and expect someone to sit there, half naked and horny, while they listen to you throw up bright yellow, acrid bile.

I should taper. Benzos can help.

Delirium tremens starts when the initial shock finishes. I don't want to die.

My chest hurts.

I don't have any alcohol at home. Can't go to Jane's pub, at least not for a bit. Got to give her a bit of space. Maybe in a week or two I can explain I was in a dark place, problems at work, explain that she was a little bit right with what she said and caught me off guard was all.

Fucksake, Coll, no. That's a stupid thing to do. That's the kind of shit which got you living alone in a shitty estate with your closest relationship being the person who serves you drinks. Who you then fucked up with. You cunt.

I don't want to have to explain my life.

I don't want to live the life I've created for myself. I don't want to die.

I know who I have to call, and it takes a fair bit of searching through my phone to find.

It's winter and there aren't any coughers sat in the GP's surgery. Got to count your blessings, I suppose. It was easy to get an appointment; they've switched to all same day stuff here. No idea who I'm seeing, but it's an

Indian-sounding name. No surprises there. Whole service is propped up by them.

My head hurts. Chest feels like it's got an elephant on it. I'm sure I'm sweating.

When I'd phoned up they'd drilled me: do I really need to see a doctor? Is it minor enough to talk to the non-emergency line, or serious enough for A&E? I'd told them that yes, I do in fact need a GP. They hadn't questioned me when I walked in. The receptionist was kind, told me to take a seat. She was older, reminded me of my mum.

When I'm done with this, she's the first one I'm calling. Never want baked beans on Christmas again.

I see my name flash up on the little LED board they have in the waiting room to save the doc actually having to come and fetch you personally. The room I'm in is upstairs. The receptionist asks if I'll be alright getting up there, and I say yes but the walk nearly kills me. Between my head, chest, and the smell of disinfectant, I think I could well collapse. At least if I do, I'm in the right place for it, right? The door is open, but I knock on it anyway.

'Mr Stephenson,' a young Indian man says. I say young, he's probably my age, but that seems young for a doctor. He's dressed Western, but still has the hint of an accent.

'Please, take a seat.'

'It's Coll, please,' I say, letting out a sad little groan as I sit.

'Of course. What can I do for you today, Coll?'

I like him. He seems nice. Here goes nothing.

I don't want to die. But I don't want to live like this, either.

'I've been having some trouble recently, doc,' I say to the

floor, hands in a ball, 'with how much I'm drinking. Been going on for a while, really. I think I need a bit of help.'

'How much would you say you drank each week?'

'A week? No idea. It varies. I tend to go day by day.'

'What would you say you drank each day, then?'

'Five or six beers. Maybe half, usually more, of a bottle of something stronger.'

'Stronger like wine?'

'No, not like wine.'

'Okay. How long would you say this has been going on for?'

'A long while. Couldn't tell you when it started. It's been better and it's been bad but it's been worse the last few months. Wasn't invited home to Christmas this year. Messed it up with a girl. I think I'm out of excuses here.'

'It's a good thing that you want to cut back on your drinking. We definitely have services here which can help you,' says the doc, a well-trained reassuring grin on his face, leaning back to start typing something on my notes. 'We have a wide range of services here – group sessions, one-on-one counselling – which will help you cut back.'

'Cut back? Doc, I'm done here. I'm looking to quit for good.'

'I understand that, Coll, but it isn't always as simple as that. Stopping drinking can be life threatening—' Delirium tremens. I know. '—and it needs to be closely monitored.'

'I know all that, I mean look at me,' I say, looking the doc dead in the eye and knowing what a pile of shit I look like, 'but I can quit. I want to. I need to, you know? But I can't handle the withdrawal. I've tried it before. I was looking for something to help with that.'

'I'm afraid I can't do that, at least not right now.'

'What? Why? I've read up on this a fair bit before coming in. Benzos, valium, it can all help have this thing not ... well, you know.'

'Do you smoke as well?'

'Yeah, probably a pack a day on average.'

'Okay,' the doc says, leaning across his desk, hands clasped. Is this fucker actually not going to help me? 'It is true, yes, that sedatives can help with the withdrawal symptoms from alcohol dependency. But you need to understand, Coll, that everything needs to be carefully monitored. By its very nature, what you have is an addiction problem, and those kinds of drugs themselves can be highly addictive. They're more used in in-patient facilities.'

'So they can help me?'

'If other things can't help you, I could look into a referral for an in-patient treatment route, but that isn't generally the first option.'

'So what can you do?'

'As I said, we offer counselling services here, both group and individually, to help you cut back and stop. They can work on a quitting plan for you, too. And I'd like to do some blood tests to check for liver function and potentially hepatitis. I'm glad you came here looking for help, but this is where we need to start.'

'Where we need to start?' I say, sitting upright and rubbing the sweaty palms of my hands on the legs of my jeans. 'I come in here, telling you I'm drinking myself half to death, that I want out of it, that I need help, and you tell me where we can start?'

'It's a long road to recovery,' he says, 'and it is never as simple as just reducing the withdrawal symptoms.'

'Nah, mate,' I say, standing up, 'you said it yourself. You think I'm just an addict. That – what – I'll come in here with puppy dog eyes looking for a different drug every week. You don't care that three times in the last two days, I've been throwing up bile. That I've chased off the last person who gives a shit about me. That I ran out of fucking drink the other night, so had to sweat and shake until dawn and the shops opened.'

'I do care, Coll, but it isn't as simple as—'

'Oh, fucking save it,' I say, walking towards the door. I put my hand on the knob but didn't leave just yet. 'So is this really your plan? Somebody asks for help, and you send them packing back home to have another drink?'

'It may not seem it now,' the doc says, himself standing up, though not moving out from behind his desk, 'but this is what will help you in the long run.'

'Fuckin' save it. Where do you think I'd get the time off work from anyway to keep coming in for blood tests and talks? I just want this over with, and if you won't help me, fine,' I say, twisting the door handle and storming off down the hallway.

Fuck him, arrogant young prick. He's got no clue. No idea. He might be able to tell the local worryguts for the third time in a week that he doesn't have cancer, or explain to some private schoolgirl's mum just why he isn't prescribing antibiotics for a cough, but show him a real problem – a person who really needs help – and he's fucking useless. But he'll take his six figures and fuck off back to Kingston or Richmond to tell his mates at dinner parties how he works in a shitty area and collect the applause.

As I walk through reception the lady behind the counter shouts out at me to wait, that the doctor is coming down to try and catch me before I leave, but I keep going. They're not going to help. Come in and talk a few times a week? Fucking great, I'll fit that in around shift work no sweat. Idiot.

I need a clear head. I can do this. Fuck him, I'll walk back into his office in a few weeks, showered and suited and shaven with a haircut, and remind him of the shaking, sweating wretch he turned away, refused to help. Show him how I've done it all by myself, make him rethink for the next time he turns someone away because they drink and smoke so he thinks they'll become a pill head too. Maybe after that I can go back to Jane, make a point of ordering a coffee, show her that she just caught me on a bad week was all, that I'm not that person, least I won't be that person any more, and I'll earn that second chance. Give her the good and stable life she deserves. Fuck those stupid fantasies of staying up all night drinking and fucking, it'll be the real thing. If it gets too much with work I can phone in sick, fuck it, I could probably even quit; without needing to piss so much money up against the wall I can get a job I'll actually enjoy. Keep regular hours. Be normal. Get anchored.

But I need a clear head. When I stop my grand exit from the doc's, I realise how shit I still feel. My vision blurs in sync with my heartbeat, chest feels like lead too. I need a plan on how to get out of this, but can't do it if I can't see a page to write it down on.

There's a corner shop on the walk back from the doc's. I'll swing in, get a bottle of Jack, some Coke, maybe a few beers for when I don't need the whiskey any more. Go home, write up a plan. Distract myself. Start tapering. Get better. But first I need to do something to finish feeling like this.

Fix

'So you're good to look after him, yeah?' Emma asks me, not really paying attention and instead checking her hair in the mirror. Her boss from Tesco's had called and said they needed someone extra on the tills this afternoon, and we needed the money.

''Course, love, stop worrying about it and get to work,' I say to her, eyes back on the telly. It's just one of those shitty American sitcoms they repeat all day long, but I hadn't seen it and it was alright.

'Three o'clock at the school gates, yeah? I phoned and said it'd be you who was picking Jackie up. They're well funny about it.' She tried her hair in a different way, trying to see if she could tie it up and not show off her roots too bad.

'I'm his dad, it's fucking ridiculous.'

'I know that, but you know the kind of sorts who're out there. I'll be back about eight.'

'It's fine, love, honest. I'll give him his tea and get him in the bath and stuff.'

Emma gives us a kiss on the top of the head as she heads out the door. I swear, she makes it out like I've got no clue how to handle the kid. He's mine, isn't he? I'm around. Usually Emma works the morning shifts if she's in during the week so she's back in time to pick him up. I'll do weekends fine, usually around with Mum or something, and yeah, mostly I've got help with him but I know what I'm doing. She makes it out like one night away from the pub'll kill me.

I know what this is all about really; she doesn't trust me. Still. It's stupid. Got in a bit of bother one time, and it was ages ago anyway, and she still gets all funny about it.

The TV show goes to a break and I flick through the channels. It's noon, got nowt to do for best part of three hours apart from sit on my arse. Only signed on a few days ago, sent the week's worth of job applications in, so I'm golden.

Nothing's holding my attention, just the usual mix of daytime bollocks: antiques shit, more repeats of American stuff, and those talk shows where absolute scummers come out to see if the missus has been fucking someone behind their back, or to try and deny being a dad. Flick across one and there are the horses on. I should move on, shouldn't be watching this stuff, but my finger hovers across the button and doesn't hit next.

Looks like a good bunch. Just a handicap on the flat, but they look lively. I don't catch their names but like the look of one already. Small, so will have a fair bit of weight on him, but just looking real calm like. The others are bucking a bit, fighting to go in their stalls, but this one trots right on in. It's a winner, can call it straight off. You can just tell when you've watched them as much as I have; previous runs and records don't mean shit. You can put a good horse out at a canter in shit, low prize money races to get them used to the ground and starts, and it skews their stats.

The bunch are set off and I turn the volume up a bit. The horse I like, with its jockey in a red check bib, is sat nice in the middle. Hear the commentator call it Shelby Supreme, sat nice in the middle of the pack. It starts moving through the field real nice too, head still straight and the jockey not needing to whip it, and it gets to the inside pulling out of the last bend. The jockey unleashes then, and the rides which bolted early are easily reeled in. Shelby Supreme wins by a length and a bit. When the graphic shows up to confirm the bloody horse was a 40/1 outsider. It trounced the lot of them.

I used to be real good at spotting horses. A lot of afternoons spent in bookies, watch a lot of races with the old boys, you notice things. I lost my eye a little, got into a bit of trouble not having many winners for a stretch, but it'd been an age. I could have put a cheeky fiver on that horse, knew it was a winner, and picked up an easy £200. More than Emma would make at work today. She wouldn't have even had to go in, could've been at home with the kid.

I flick the telly off when I see the next race start to get ready. The horses are a dangerous thing; sport of kings alright but they can make a right fool out of everyone else. I need to get outside. Got two and a bit hours and I can't sit and look at the horses. Triggers, the wanker Emma made me go and talk to, called them. Makes you not be able to say no, like a fag when you're having a drink. I know it too, any more time sat on the sofa and I'll have the laptop out. Instead I get me coat on and go for a walk around town.

It's grey and spitting but I don't care. I light up a cig on the doorstep and think about that horse. I knew it. Could have done with that money for winning it, I was stupid not to trust myself. Fucksake. I need to clear my head. This isn't a trigger bullshit or whatever they try to call it, I've got experience and I knew it. I should have bet on it, now I'm basically £200 out of pocket for not.

I start walking towards town and get a plan going in my head. I can't get silly with money, Emma's told me it's last chance saloon with that shit. I need to budget, that's what I need to do. I've got a hundred quid or so in my account, and I sign on again next week so I'll get a bit more then. If I pop down to the cashpoint and get things out I can see what I've got and I can budget it out. That'll help. It's a good plan.

I light up another snout for the walk and get going. If I can just get to the cashpoint I'll know what I can spend each day, figure it out, and it'll stop me being silly. It's good. It's accountability and stuff. It's what Emma wanted to hear from me. She was getting better too, surprised me by giving me one of those pricey iPhones that can go on the internet and stuff to show she did. Not going to fuck around with that trust, nah. This'll stop me being silly.

I check the account and I can take a hundred and ten out. Few quid left in, but banks haven't clocked that people are hard up yet so don't let you take fivers out. Got nine days until I need to sign on again, so that's about twelve quid a day; three pints and a Polish pack that the guy who runs the corner shop keeps under the counter for people he knows. Easy. Might have a few quid left over to play the fruity, just to see what's what. I could pop in now for a beer or two, see if any of the locals are in for a chat. This time of day there might be a few builders in over lunch, and they can't help but chuck their money into a fruity.

Shouldn't think this way. It's dangerous. Plus, there's no point to playing the fruities in the pub anyway. Most you'll get is a ton. But that only happens once in a blue moon. You want the real money you've got to play the big ones down at the services, but Emma's got the car to get into work and I've still got to retake my test anyway. The slots down the bookies can pay out big, they've got to pay out ninety-seven per cent of the time. It's the law. Used to be easier when you could still play roulette down there, but even after the changes you can still get a good run going and be laughing.

This is stupid. I shouldn't be doing this, told Emma I wouldn't be any more. Not after the trouble. But missing out on that free cash on the horse burns me right up inside. That would have been class. Could have really treated her and the kid to something.

I can't pop to the pub and put the change in the fruity today because of the kid – bad look to go to the school from the pub – but could just go to the bookies now instead. The corner shop is just across the street, could get a tinny and some cigs and then have a few spins on the slots. If I dipped into tomorrow and another day's money – probably won't go out both nights this weekend or whatever, or could do away with popping down for a pint on the weekend while Mum watches Jackie – then I'd have enough for a solid couple of spins. Won't lose everything each time, of course, so can see how we're doing there. Emma won't know, and

I'll win something and be able to surprise her. She just wants me to be sensible. This is sensible.

I have the last snout from the pack as I walk around to the corner shop. Been a walk I've done a bare amount, and I got the timing down, chucking the butt into the street as I walk in. The door thing beeps and I get a twinge of excitement, some proper Pavlov shit. Always come in for a tinny before I go across the road to the Paddy Power. It's the start of it. I get a single can of Tuborg and a pack from below the counter. Back on the street I slip the tin into my coat pocket and light another cigarette. It's the start of things.

I smoke this one real slow to draw it all out. It's a part of it all. Inside things can go so quick, it can be over before you know it's happened, or had a chance to enjoy it. This slows everything down. Ritual like. Footballers and tennis players do it before they go out and play. I exhale through my nose after each drag, enjoying the taste of them. Smoke it right down to the butt, close as you can without getting the harsh burn of the filter, before crossing the road and heading into the shop. Used to be a butcher's when I was a kid but since everyone started just going to the big out-of-town shop it was empty for ages. Paddy Power moved in a few years back, so at least people go there again, even if it is mainly old boys hanging out with little half bottles of Scotch for most of the day. Still, lot of people go to play the machines. Used to be roulette, but now they've changed all that and it's slots. Don't really matter, though, I like them however they come. Used to do okay on the old ones before I had a shitty bad luck run.

Was a real kick that that happened the same time as I lost my knack with the horses.

I go into the shop and it's the same young Indian lad behind the counter. He's a bit simple, but not bad.

'Y'alright, mate? Haven't seen you in a while,' he says to me.

'Yeah, not bad, ta. You doing okay?' I say back, not exactly bothered but it's all a part of the ritual.

'Yeah, not bad. You know how it is.'

I give him a nod and head to my favourite machine down the back of the shop, right in the corner. As I walk past the old boys I give them nods too. Don't really know them but used to see them in The Falcon when I was still at school. The landlord there ran a dodgy bookies from behind the bar, back in the day when you had proper pubs that used to do that kind of thing instead of the chain shit with cheap drinks you get now. Not that I mind the cheap drinks, 'course. The old boys've got a few slips in front of them now, having a flutter on the horses, and I might join them when I'm done with the slots. Still sore about that horse this morning, but this is the safer option. Won't get carried away with it. Can win some of the money I should have earlier, no sweat.

I settle down at my favourite machine and crack open my tinny, taking a long drink. It's a bit warm 'cause the shop has shit fridges, but it's beer so fuckit. The cashpoint gave us crisp new tenners, and I feed two of them into the machine after I load up the game I like, themed after knights and queens and the animation is alright. Either way, I've only put in enough for ten spins, then I'll see where I'm at. Won't touch the ultra feature, lets you play a mini-game with less chances but much quicker and more cash up for grabs. At least not until I think it'll hit. It's funny, nowadays I think I'll use a little two-quid spin tactically and back in the day I'd easily have thirty laid out. Could never afford it, had to use those payday loan people and couldn't pay them back a few times after a few bad spins, so now I'm sensible and take my time on the small spins.

When it asks me to set my limits I bump them up to the max – if you don't they just bug you – and start my little baby spins. First few don't really do anything, and when I only hit a few lines I skip the animation: don't need all the ceremony to watch you pay me out twenty p, ta. I take a sip of my beer and slip another tenner in. Bit cheeky of me but I don't want the balance to get too low and the machine to reset. Plus you're supposed to up your stake if you lose, called the Martingale system, read about it online. Machine's holding steady well, going to pay out big, I can feel it, or at least put me through into one of the big-money mini-games. If the balance gets too low it'll think that I've stopped and a new player has come in. Everything'll reset and I'll lose what I've put in, you see.

I reach into my wallet again, just to keep the balance healthy. I reach in again when I try a few of the rapid-fire ultra-feature games but come up dry. Ideal amount to have is about twelve quid, I think. Low enough that the machine wants to pay you to keep playing, but high enough that if you have a couple of bad spins you aren't screwed. And the cash is getting close too, I can feel it. They always tighten up before they pay out, just got to ride the storm. Wasn't going to put another tenner in but this is going right down to the wire. Balance has dropped and needs a refill. I reach into my wallet one more time to fish out another tenner to keep it healthy and I just rub against the cloth inside. I look down and it's empty.

Fuck. Had I lost count?

I need to win that money back. Should have bet on the horse this morning. Should have trusted myself, just stuck a cheeky twenty on it, and be sat at home laughing with £800 waiting to surprise Emma and Jackie with a little holiday or something. Would have been so much simpler instead of having to do this shit.

Need to win that money back. I need a few quid between now and sign on and I can't let on to Emma that I had a bit of a wobble, she'll fucking kill me. Plus the machine hasn't gone back to the main screen yet, still knows it's me here playing, so I need to move fast.

Next to the debit card in my wallet is the credit card that Emma got us for emergencies with Jackie. Let me have a card to it same time she gave me the iPhone. I can use it to win the money back, then log onto the bank thing from my phone and pay it all off. It'll be all blessed.

All the machines have got card swipes on them so you don't even really need cash, but it doesn't like the card I'm using. I try it a few times and each time it flashes up an error. The slot machine goes back to the menu and I swear to myself; might have reset. Need to be quick. I go over to the lad behind the counter.

'Think there's something up with that machine,' I tell him, 'doesn't like my card.'

'You got money on it?' he asks as he holds his hand out, as if he'll be able to magically figure out what's wrong with it.

'Yeah, it's got a big limit and nothing on there.' I'm getting well anxious, just takes one person to waltz up to my machine and put a jammy few quid in and it's all for shit.

'This a debit or credit card?' the lad asks.

'Credit.'

'That's your problem, machines don't take them.'

'That's fucking stupid,' I say, real quick before I can catch myself. I stop and breathe; got to be calm here, can't act like an idiot. 'Isn't there anything you can do?' I ask.

'Nah, not up to us, it's a government thing. Can't use credit cards in here to gamble, meant to stop people getting in trouble with money.'

'Great,' I say, mainly to myself. The fuck am I going to do?

I go outside and light a snout to consider my options. On the one hand I could try using the credit card in a cashpoint, but they give you massive charges for that shit. Can't use the payday loan things any more either; got in enough trouble with them. Been blacklisted, and the ones who will still loan me are the proper fuck-you-and-your-kneecaps types.

Check my phone and realise that I'm supposed to be picking the kid up in an hour. Can't do that, got to sort this shit out. I pull the phone out, dial up Mum.

'Y'alright, love?' she says after a few rings.

'Yeah, good, ta. I know it's short notice but can you do us a favour? I need you to pick Jackie up from school. You around?'

'Sure, love. Everything alright if Emma isn't going down?'

'Yeah, it's golden. She's had to go into work and cover a shift, and I was going to pick him up but I've got to pop down to The Falcon. One of the guys said they might know someone who needs a bit of help on jobs, might get some odd days' work out of it.'

'Oh, that's good, love. Sure, I can go over and pick him up.'

'Great. I should be over to pick him up well before dinner, but in case I'm not can you get him his tea?'

'Yeah, I think I've got stuff in the freezer, shouldn't be a problem,' she says. I can tell what she means is she'll have to stop and get something just in case, but right now I've got bigger problems.

I say thanks again and hang up, back to the problem at hand. I get a flash of excitement and stick my hands in my pockets; know what I'm going to do. It's a shit-awful plan, but I haven't got any more options. Need to sort this mess out. Get some money back, just enough to scrape through until next week's sign on, then that'll be the end of it. Can't have Emma know this is going on.

I light another snout – need to slow down there, can't buy any more just yet – and get a move on. Keep telling myself that so long as I'm back quick, the machine'll be okay. It has to pay out ninety-seven per cent of the time, that's the law, and if it's just eaten a hundred-odd from me it's well due to pay. It'll just be the old boys putting quids on big accas in there for another hour or two, sure of it. I'll have a bit of time before the builders and office boys turn up and try to rinse the machines.

Day has turned proper grey and rainy, and I wish I brought my coat out now. Feel bad for making Mum go out in it but I need to fix this.

I don't hang about outside Cash Converters and go straight in. It's one of the big ones; shop itself is actually kind of small, but it's got a big sorting area in the back. It's the way the world works, poor fuckers like us can't afford the nice shit we buy so we sell it, then they ship it off to sell cut-price in better-off areas. Disgusting, but still need to get seen and sorted real quick like.

'Course there is only one bloke on and there's a mum in front with her kid running riot. She's having a barny with the bloke about why he won't take her stuff – it's old tapes and kid stuff her little one has grown out of or got bored of – which is going to be absolutely bloody worthless, and they don't buy stuff like that anyway. She's not having it, though, giving him a right ear-load about how he thinks she's dirty or something, she's sold loads of stuff here before, all of that. She's not leaving, I'm in a hurry, and he's trying to talk her down, and all the while her kid is causing fuckin' mayhem with anything on the shelves. He tells her to go and look after her kid and she grabs him stiffly by the arm, making him cry. I meet eyes with her when she turns around and she's strung out; glazed eyes and cheekbones you could slice a tomato on.

He pushes the box of random shit she brought in to try and flog and recommends she either try a car boot sale or just donate it. She calls him a cunt and tucks it under one arm, walking out with it and dragging her kid along. As she turns the box bashes into me and I tell her to watch it. She tells me to fuck off, and I have a mumble to myself about fucking skag-heads around town.

'Sorry about that,' the bloke behind the counter says to me when I walk up. I can tell he's still fuming and doesn't want to deal with me, but I'm alright and I'll be good to him.

'Idiots, mate. Sorry you've got to deal with 'em.'

'Used to only get one or two like that a week, now you're lucky to only get one a day.'

The bloke looks out the front door behind me, and I do a quick check. The young mum has dropped the box and all her crap is over the street. She's just yelling at her kid for it, who in turn sits down on the wet pavement having a tantrum. Disgusting that people like that can have kids.

'Anyway,' the guy behind the counter – Richard, his name tag says – goes to me, 'what can I help you with?'

'Just looking to see what I can get for this,' I say, pushing my phone across the counter. He picks it up and does the checks for scratches and stuff.

'You got the box and stuff for it?' he asks me.

'At home. I'm looking to do this quickly, on the buy-back option. Only going to need the money for a day or two, really.'

'Have you thought about one of the short-term loans we can offer, then? Might be better than risking your phone.'

'Nah, can't use them any more. Got to be this way.'

'For the phone without the accessories, along with the buy-back guarantee, I can only offer you £127.'

'Yeah, that's fine,' I say. But they're actually fucking rip-off merchants. That phone new from a shop would be a few hundred quid, and they'll sell it for at least £200. Got to be nice, though, he's holding the cash I need.

'Alright, can I grab your photo ID and a proof of address and I'll start processing.'

I pull my stupid green provisional licence out, and the old folded-up gas bill I keep in one of the pockets in the wallet. Seems weird to most to carry it about but when you don't have a lot of cards and credit and rely on the payday fuckers like I did, you use it a lot. Got to have money to be trusted by anyone these days. It's why I hate having to give him my ID, he's only checking I haven't thieved the thing, like I'm no better than the skag-head, fuck-up mum who was in with her poor brat earlier.

'Alright,' Richard says, suddenly a bit nicer now he's confirmed I'm pawning my own phone and not one I got off some kid in the park or whatever he thinks I might be capable of, 'I can put this into testing now. There's a bit of a backlog, end of the month and all that, so it'll probably be ready about lunchtime tomorrow?'

What? Nah, fuck that.

'Yeah, that's not really any good for me at all, mate,' I say to him, trying to stay nice. 'I really need that money short-term, you know? I'm planning on getting it back off you by the end of the day. Anything you can do?'

'I'm afraid not, everything needs to be tested to make sure it works so we can—'

'Yeah, yeah, I know that,' I say, cutting him off and stopping him talking to me like I'm as thick as a fucking sponge, 'but can you pop it in the front of the line for us? It'd be a big favour.'

'It looks pretty new anyway, give us a minute,' he says, and takes it into the back testing room. I drum on the counter, trying to keep calm and stop images of people rinsing out my machine. That thing is going to pay out big, give me all the reels I need, I just need to get back there.

'Had a word,' Richard says, popping back from outside the back room sans phone, 'and they'll do it now quickly. Looks in good nick so shouldn't be any issues. Be about half an hour.'

'Great, cheers,' I say to him. Fucksake, though, half an hour? I go outside and smoke a few butts down to the nub in the rain before entertaining myself looking at all the other nice shit on their shelves that people have had to flog to get their worlds back afloat.

By the time I'm back outside the corner shop, fresh tin of beer in my pocket and a new pack of snouts, it's been an hour. Hope nobody has been in to rinse the machine. Try and calm myself, have a cig like normal, stick to routine, but this has got to be the game of my life. Got to be real disciplined. No big gambles, got to win this back.

I step on the butt and walk across the road, back into Paddy Power. Give out nods to the old boys and the young lad behind the counter screen again before settling down to my machine. I go through all the steps – open can, sip, cash in, sip, pick game, sip – and get going. Takes a while for the reels to start coming good, have to feed a few more notes in, but soon they start coming thick and fast.

This is what I waited for, what all the shit I had to wade through today was all about. The reels start hitting, even putting me into some of the smaller jackpot games, and the balance goes up real quick. This is it, the machine spitting back my money from earlier plus a whole lot more. Way more than the few hundred I'd have won on that stupid fucking horse. This machine is about to turn into a cash-point, it's on a streak, and I start quick tapping the button to spin the reels, not hanging about to watch what each turn pays out. With the machine behaving itself I even start dipping in to the higher payout game too, subbing in five spins for every ten or so I do on the main game. It's a false economy otherwise; I want the winnings I had before while the machine is paying out, and if I wager less it'll just mean I have to gamble longer and have more time to lose it. Got to play smart.

The balance creeps above £200 and I could easily cash out, get my phone back, have this all be done, but fuck that. This day owes me something. I want that big win I didn't get earlier. I hate that Emma has to go off and do shit like work extra shifts. I'm going to clean this machine out, treat it like a fuckin' golden goose, until I get a wedge. Be able to surprise Jackie with a nice present – they had a few consoles in Cash Converters, could get the house one of them – or maybe even be able to take Emma away for a good few days. I start tapping spin faster, only interrupted to tell the limit message to fuck off; might even be able to go abroad again. Haven't done that in forever, not since before I wasn't working so much and we had Jackie.

The balance starts to dip but I'm not worried, got a load in my wallet and still well over a ton in the machine. I keep the reels spinning, not really paying attention to what they do but just hoping to get them lined up so it'll put me in a jackpot game. The machine is hot, but streaks only last for so long. After a while it'll cool off again, and then I'll be back trying to grind out a profit from small spins with only a few lines.

The balance drops to below a ton after a few spins, but I'm high stakes and this'll have one more payday in it. Mean, with enough I can maybe even put off the Job Centre wankers for a few more weeks before they make me go do something brain-killing.

The reels do cool off, and the balance drops to below fifty. Fucksake, machine is tightening up. System says to still bet big, so I start on the quickfire high returns mini-game instead of the reels. I focus in now, watching the one line of reels and waiting for one of the patterns I knew so well to flash up. This is it, now. One more good spin. One more hit. When it comes I'll cash out, get my phone, and figure out the rest tomorrow.

INSUFFICIENT FUNDS

I look up at the balance: zero. Fucking zero. House wins. Everything gone.

No, I say aloud, for fucksake, no. I smack the side of the machine, the stupid fucking thing. It knew. It understood what I was doing, how I was playing it, and fucked me. Fucksake, it's as bent as the fucking horses.

'Watch it,' I hear from the young lad behind the screen. Dull shit brick. I smack the side of it, crooked thing, knocking my tinny of the little drinks holder attached to the side they have because they want drunk fuck-ups to waste all their money on these stupid things.

'That's enough, yeah?' he says to me, still from behind his sad little counter.

'Or what?' I say, walking over. He's either in on the scam, or too thick to know. Either way he's a part of those fucking machines, robbing people of the money they need.

'Leave it, yeah? You've had a bad run, and I'm sorry, but—'

'No, you're fucking not,' I growl at him, slamming both hands against the screen they put up in front of him 'cause they're too scared to face people they've just mugged off. He steps back but one of the old boys at the horse table stands up and tells me to leave it too. I know him, he might be sixty-odd these days but there were stories of him battering people half to death for getting rowdy in The Falcon. Don't think he's needed a fight in forever, reputation does it now, and I might be mad as hell but I'm not an idiot. Instead I walk out the shop and try to slam the glass door behind me, but it's got one of those air hinges and so just rattles as it gently closes.

Fucksake. A week's worth of money and now a phone. The fuck am I going to tell Emma? She doesn't get it. Nobody gets it. Thinks when you can watch your cash disappear from your hand you've got to be a proper idiot to keep pissing it away in those fucking machines. It's not like that, though.

It's like a night out on the piss, yeah? You have a few drinks, have a few laughs, and you get to the point where you know you're already going to feel dead dog rough the next morning but you say to hell with it, this is the time of my fucking life. This thirst comes over you. You keep drinking because you think if you stop, sit out a round, you'll sober up, the fun will stop, and you're back to real life. You talk deep and you talk bullshit and you talk about all the ways you want your life to be better and you think of ways to get out there and do it. It lights this fire inside you. Maybe when the night is over you stagger back, pour yourself one of those home measure drinks which is basically just a glass of whiskey or vodka or whatever you've got laying around with a splash of Coke in to make it look like you're at least trying to ease off. You sit on your front doorstep and drink and chain-smoke cigarettes and think of all the ways which your life is going to be better now that you've figured shit out. You've broken the back of the beast thanks to the monkey on yours and the future is only going to get better. You might pour another and then one more and then the sky starts to stain purple as the sun comes up, streetlights blending into it as it gets lighter and lighter and you think, nah, maybe I won't even go to bed, I feel fucking alive and I know what I want to do. But it's five in the morning and the world won't be up and about until eight or nine so you think, alright, I'm not that pissed, I'll get a few hours kip and set an alarm and then up-and-fucking-at-them.

Then you wake up a few hours later, glass of spirit by your bed and a bit of food you don't remember even cooking spilled on the sheets, and spend the rest of the day sweating and chucking up bile. The high has gone, and now your hung-over arse has to deal with the fact that it was all an illusion; you might have wanted to fucking change your life, change everything about it, and seen an out, but really it's been chasing that out which has fucked you up beyond all belief. You swear off it and try to get yourself better, but you know the next week you'll be chasing the dreams in the bottoms of pint glasses again.

This is my hangover.

I smoke another cig on the walk home and stick my head in through the front door. Need to figure out a plan before – was that a car pulling up outside? I crane my head around the front window and sure enough, Emma is back home. It's barely five, she shouldn't be back for three hours.

Shit.

I try and act relaxed as she gets in.

'Y'alright, love, back early?' I say, but she blanks me and shuts the door.

'Where's Jackie?' she asks. She's pissed, her voice all flat. She knows he's not here, it's not a question she's really asking.

'At Mum's,' I say, 'I'd have phoned you but you were working. Didn't think they'd let you have it out.'

'Want to know how I know she's at your mum's? Because the school had to phone me at work. Not just on my mobile, but the actual shop.'

'I didn't think it'd matter, I'm sorry, babe,' I say. Literally no clue schools were so paranoid these days.

'Where were you?' she asks, staring me down.

'I got a call from one of the lads down The Falcon. Said his site needed a few more lads to work, casual like. Apparently, the Poles were just fucking off when they could get a few extra quid a day somewhere else, no loyalty that lot. Don't know if it's a goer, but might be.'

'I've been calling you, after that,' she says, real fucking

cold. No trust, she's got. 'Keeps going to voicemail straight off. Texts aren't going through neither.'

I pat my pockets. Hate this bit of the act.

'Shit, must've left it at the pub. If it's off it's probably been turned off and put behind the bar for us. I'll nip up tomorrow and grab it, or maybe swing by on the way to get Jackie. Mum said she'd sort him out tea if needs be. We could even make the best of an empty house,' I say, moving closer to her and going to put my hands on her waist.

'Fuck off,' she shouts, 'just fuck off. Don't touch me.'

'Why are you being like this? I'm sorry for leaving my phone somewhere, yeah?'

'Why are you lying to me?' she says, and I hold her eyes.

You're supposed to raise your stake when you lose your bet, aren't you?

'I'm not, love. Told you, I don't do that shit any more.'

'Then why,' she says, real slow and rehearsed, 'when I was checking my voicemails from your mum and the school, did I find one from the bank?'

'The bank?' I say. Genuinely lost on me.

'Their fraud lot. If you get a credit card declined they phone, you fucking idiot. You used it at Paddy Power.'

'No, I . . .' I start to say, but I've hit zero. I got nothing. They phone you? Fucksake.

Thought I could at least have tomorrow to try to sort all this shit out.

'Just go,' she says, 'just fuck off and go. I'm done. I told you you didn't have any more chances, and you go and do this stupid stuff.'

'Look, no, it was just a little mistake. A wobble. It won't

happen again, will it, eh?' I say and reach an arm out towards her, but she bats it down.

'Fuck off,' she says again, 'get out. I'm going to go and pick Jackie up, give us your key.'

I hand it over. She always gets in a mood like this, it's a part of my hangover. 'Have we got to do this now? I'm sorry. Why don't I go and get Jackie and we'll talk—'

'I told you,' she snaps, not meeting my eyes any more 'cause hers are so suddenly red, 'once more and we're done. We can't go on like this.'

'What about all my stuff?'

'What about your fucking kid? The one you dumped off so you could piss whatever money you've got away. Just go.'

I need to let her calm down. There's no reasoning with her like this. I feel as fucking shit as anyone about today; it's embarrassing. And she wants to turf me out? Fuck that.

'Fine, I'll call you tomorrow,' I say, and hear her say 'How?' as I get to the door. I slam it. This one works.

Fuck her. I messed up. She made me go to those courses to learn all those fancy fucking words like 'triggered', and as soon as I am she turfs me out. It's stupid. I light a snout and inhale harsh, power walking down the street. No idea where to. This is one bad fucking hangover.

I want a pint but I've got no money. Mum's always good for a tenner and a sofa. I should head around there; give her a call and warn her I'm heading round, give her a heads-up that Emma will be coming around pissed off and spewing shit too. They don't like each other at the best of times. I should get in touch, maybe text around a few mates to try and sort something out. Got a feeling this one might take a while to smooth over. Could see if any of them are free to go down The Falcon, sure I'll get a few beers bought to ease the pain of having the missus turf me out.

I stick my hand in my pocket to give Mum a call, but . . . oh, for fucksake.

Exams

Didn't think I'd actually be nervous, it all went down years ago. We'd moved on; different people, different lives, all of that. We were kids then. I used to be a proper idiot and she didn't know any better either, both of us figuring shit out. Still, I'm fucking bricking it as I walk down the high street on the way to pre-game it at the house. It's cold and dingy, cheap orange streetlights shining off the greasy-looking ground. Got one hand stuffed into my coat pocket, other one turning into a frozen claw as it clutches a carrier bag holding some beers and a shit-cheap bottle of sparkly.

Danno had called soon as he saw.

'Ay, Grant bruv, you seen that Abs is coming to Kim's birthday thing at the weekend? You gonna be able to be all cool with it, yeah?'

I played it dumb and shrugged it off but, yeah, obviously, I had seen. We still had mutuals all these years later and hadn't taken each other off our Facebooks fully, so it'd told me she clicked she was going. I'd poked around her profile to see what was new too; did that sometimes, nothing creepy about it but just to see if she had any new pictures up and check she hadn't taken me off it fully. Never liked anything or nothing, just looked. She had a new profile pic up which annoyed me as I loved her old pic; used to be an arty one of her in a little black bikini on some beach from her travels, big sun hat on looking out over the ocean. Looked like a dream, and sexy as fuck. The shame was her latest upload was one of her at some fancy dinner thing in a white dress, next to that tall, rowing fuck.

I get to Kim's place – well, her mum's, she still lives at home and pushes trollies down at Tesco's with Danno – and can hear the music and chatter through the door. I ring the bell and when there's no answer give the door a knock. She looks a bit of a state when she answers it, inch of slap on and spilling out of a pink dress a few sizes too small.

'Y'alright,' I say as I pull the cheap bubbly out of the bag, 'happy birthday.'

'Aww, thanks, love,' she says, cooing at the bottle. Before she reaches out to take it she holds the bottom of her dress and shimmies her hips side to side to attempt to pull it back down. Someone's got to tell her to change, she's put on a bit and it's embarrassing.

'Come on in.'

Everyone's in the kitchen so I crack a beer and have a chat. There are a few I don't know, guess it's Kim's work-mates, but some of the lads from school are here too and I have a catch-up. Danno is in the corner with a bottle of Jack and a bottle of Coke. He's not mixing it, just taking a swig then washing it down.

'You good, fam?' he asks after ripping a shot.

'Yeah, all blessed.'

'You sure?' he asks again, holding my eyes.

''Course, mate.'

There's no Abs. Perhaps she won't come, it'll all be a lot of stress for nothing. People say they're coming, it's clicking a button and looking polite, it's nothing. No means no, maybe means no, yes means maybe. Still, I'm disappointed. Not given time to think about it.

'How you doing, Grant?' Kim asks me, the fizzy stuff poured into a pint glass, 'work treating you alright?'

'It's not bad,' I say between sips, 'put me up the pay grade a year or so ago. Should be able to ask for another one soon. So yeah, it's alright.'

'You still at that call centre?' she asks, and it rubs me the wrong way.

'Yeah. I mean, I work senior now. Don't actually answer the phones. But yeah.'

She can't see the difference and tells me it's nice. Now, I know she means nothing by it but, still, I worked hard to get there, man, and just 'cause you're still working minimum don't mean I am. I ask where I can smoke and she nudges her head towards the sliding doors at the little back garden-cum-patio affair. There are a couple of Kim's workmates out there smoking shit and having a chat, but I'm not feeling it and instead look at my phone. I try and look concerned, like I'm all important, got an urgent work email or something, but it's just so I don't have to make small talk. The group go back in and I put my phone away; can't hold a phone, fag, and beer all at once. A few of Kim's mates look alright, I should look to get back on with the night.

I come back in and try to make eyes with Danno, and he's rolling up a joint. Fuckin' perfect.

'You got any going, mate?' I ask him, but he doesn't talk about that.

'Bruv,' he says, and nods his head towards the kitchen. 'Be cool, yeah.'

Her hair is different. She used to cut it short, too short I'd think, short and scruffy like she aimed for the pixie look but missed, instead looking more like a lad whose mum did a scissor cut at home to save a few quid. She told me how much she hated her hair, ginger and brittle like straw that somehow sat flat and fuzzy all at once. Think I told her to just wear a hat, then. But it was longer now, wavy and thick down past her shoulders. Not ginge any more either, but a deep dark red that stood out against her black dress. I'd seen it in the photos I'd looked at on her socials, but they looked like dogshit compared to seeing her in person. She was wearing heels, she'd never worn heels when she'd been with me.

'Cuz,' Danno says to me, 'you're staring. C'mon, let's smoke this.'

Danno leads me back outside, and as I get to the sliding doors I can't help but take a look at her. The two girls she must've come with – sad as it is, I know they're her uni mates, recognise them from photos, and she travelled with one of them – are introducing themselves to Kim. Chatting about what a shitshow the club'll be later. Abs isn't a part of it, and I see her pull her dress down slightly, then use the arm which isn't holding a wine glass across herself. She looks up, and for a split second I think she looks over at me. Before I can find out if she has I slip outside and close the door, not looking back through.

Danno offers a hit off his jay and I don't really do it no more but right now it feels like just what I need. I cough a bit but not as much as I should and enjoy the taste of it, was like sunny days down by the river, bunking off of school to have a few zutes.

I start to feel alright. Danno chats some useless shit to me to take my mind off her, and the couple of beers I've had start to hit me. Might've just been the one drag of the jay, Danno always had some supersonic shit. We go back in and a few more have arrived so now there's twenty-odd in the small open-plan downstairs of Kim's gaff. It's getting crowded and the general chit-chat is drowning out the little Bluetooth speaker she's got trying its hardest in the corner. Kim tries to get everyone's attention by standing on the kitchen table, but all she achieves is turning her face a deeper shade of pink than her too-small dress. Someone shouts out that they can see her arse but she doesn't care and slaps it instead. Starts to get people's attention.

'Oi, listen up, yeah?' she shouted, wobbling back and forth and trying in vain again to shimmy her dress down. From somewhere she'd found a cheap tatty Poundland sash that said 'Birthday Gurl'.

'Listen, we're about to go out, yeah?' she shouts, having most people's attention, 'we're about to go out and get fucking smashed, but let's all have a drink first, yeah?'

Behind her I see Abs and one of her uni friends pouring sparkly into plastic cups for everyone. It's the same shitty kind I'd bought Kim. Fuckit, who cares, we're all here now. Kim picks up a bottle with half left in it that wouldn't fit in the plastic cups and slurs as she tells everyone to not drink until she says. Abs and her uni mate go around passing drinks out, and I make sure to take one from her mate. When I do she looks at me sideways and gives me a weird half smile. She knows who I am, probably because Abs told her about the local lad who was her first love and stuff, and I know who she is because I still can't help but look at Abs' photos.

'Alright, yeah, let's smash a good one!' Kim shouts as she leads people in downing their drinks. I do my best to drink the bubbly but it's warm and somehow too sharp and too sweet all at once. Still, though, it's a drink.

Danno has to lift Kim down from off the counter and he does so with a big cheeky grin. She's had a thing for him for years and loves the attention, and I know Danno's definitely wound up linking with her more than once after a night out. Early signs say it'll happen again tonight. Once Kim's back on solid ground she starts herding cats to try and get everyone to do the walk to the local club. It takes an age; people fucking around thinking if they'll need coats, can they leave shit here if they're coming back around after, popping to the loo and touching up make-up. I take a beer and stand out front on the street so as to try and make sure people do head that way. I'm looking down the street and people inside take long enough for me to finish my drink, so I think about nipping back inside and grabbing another. I look back at the house and can swear I see Abs and her friends start to come back outside before shuffling back in. Probably got called in from someone I didn't hear. I have a smoke instead of another drink. Halfway through the butt the main flood of people come out the front door and I let myself get swept up in it.

It's fucking bitter out but I'm glad I didn't bother with a coat because all I'll have to do is carry it about inside or pay a rip-off amount to check it in. Besides, on the walk home I'll have a proper Irish coat on anyway. I'm walking up front with Kim and Danno, leading the drunks to the promised land as the main gaggle follows. I look over my shoulder and notice Abs and her friends hanging at the back, but that makes sense because Abs only really knows Kim – they'd been best mates for years, think their mums or dads are friends or something – and her mates only know Abs – so makes sense.

It's about half-ten when we get to Winks – place has had half a dozen names over the years and hasn't actually been Winks for an age, but that's the name that stuck with us 'cause it's what it was when we all turned eighteen – and we all know it's early. Place'll be mostly empty as it doesn't really fill up until The Falcon kicks out in an hour or so, and fuck going there. Free before eleven, too. Kim knows how to organise a good night and figured if we head here earlier then we could find a little area to dump coats and make our own without having to pay for a booth. What the fuck kind of shitbag local club charges for a booth, anyway?

When we get up to the bouncers they're mostly hanging around chatting and it feels like we're bothering them by asking us to be let in. It's the usual shit with IDs out, check the girls' bags and pat the blokes down for knives. I used to resent it when I was younger but now at least they check everyone. We start to wander through but I hang back to make sure that everyone gets in drama free because it's an absolute nightmare when half of you head in and then one person has forgotten their ID or is on a bouncer's shitlist or something. I watch as Abs takes her turn to get processed and all of a sudden the bouncers look a bit perkier.

'How you doing tonight, love?' one of them asks. He's a big lad, easily six-four and looks like he splits his time between the gym and getting shit tattoos.

'Yeah, good thanks,' Abs says to him, brushing a bit of hair back behind her ear.

'What brings you out here tonight?'

'It's my friend's birthday,' she says as the bouncer takes a close look at her ID.

'Well, I hope you have a good night with us, Abigail,' the bouncer says with a smile as he hands it back. Fuck, she hates being called that. Always has done, why I call her Abs.

'Thanks, I hope so too. I haven't been back here since this place was Winks, and that was years ago. At least before I went to uni.'

'It's much nicer now, I promise you.'

'Can't be worse. I know, I worked here for a bit, too.'

'Someone like you working here? I don't believe it.'

'It was just for a year,' she says with a giggle and a tuck of hair behind the ear. 'Had to do an extra exam to get onto the uni course I wanted and needed to do something.'

'Well, let me know what you think of the improvements on the way out. Maybe we'll tempt you back here sooner rather than later.'

'I will, and let's see,' she says with a smile.

She takes her ID and waits for her friends, and when I see they're all going to be let in fine I head inside and upstairs to track down Danno and Kim. They're at the bar to the surprise of precisely no one, him with a beer and her holding a cocktail that probably has more sugar than drink in it. They've got me a beer too, and shots for all three of us. I take it and it is absolutely fucking vile. I need a swig of beer to try and rid the taste of it, and as I swing around I see Abs heading towards one of the other bars. Fuckit, she'll come over when she's ready. We haven't seen each other since we broke up five-odd years ago now, it's got to be a lot for her.

I get on with dancing and drinking and try to put Abs out of my mind but I can't. We got a lot of history, me and Abs, and maybe it's harder for her to shake it and just come say hello. I know she has her new rowing fuck boyfriend but we had that young love thing going on. She was the year below me at school and we were together right the way up from the end of her Year 10 until she did her main exams. I know her family didn't like me because we used to hang out down the rec and drink and smoke on the swings a bit, and she never used to do that, but to be fair what else is there to even do around here? Reckon they must've got to her in the end. After it went down it took her a while to get over it because she hung around for another year – working here, as she'd said to the bouncer – because things got rough towards the end, they do before things end, but we'd been each other's firsts in every way. Alright, fine, I'd had a few things but she was the first one I was with proper, where we explored and shit. You don't forget your firsts, you'd think she wouldn't be in such a hurry to forget me.

The dance floor is filling out as more people make their way over, and the couple of extra drinks are beginning to hit me and all. I look around for Abs' red hair but can't see it anywhere. I'm warm and stuffy and don't have any prospects on the dance floor so I look to go and head outside to the smoking area, you can usually spark up a chat out there. The one at Winks is pretty alright too, on the second floor on a balcony. You can't take drinks outside here because too many daft cunts have glassed each other, and so I drain my pint and look around for Danno to see if he wants to come. Him and Kim are back in a corner, though, looking like they were ready to jump each other so I head out solo.

I was glad I didn't have my coat on me as the wave of cold air that hit me when I finally stepped outside was pure fucking bliss. Before I spark up I stand there with my head rolled back taking big, deep, beautiful lungfuls of thick cold air as drizzle falls on my face. I swear my head must've been steaming like the metal covers to the red smoking lights. It's only when some other bloke needs to get past to head back inside that I come back to reality and shuffle into the smoking area proper. There are a few tables out here with people sat around them but it's not too crowded, I'm happy to just stand by the balcony edge and watch the entrance below as The Falcon lot make their way weaving up the high street. It's only when I look over behind to see where the nearest ashtray is so I don't just chuck it on the floor that I clock the sea of deep red hair, and we meet eyes proper for the first time. She holds my look for a little and I shoot her a smile, but she turns away and angles back in towards her little group of friends until I can just see her toned back.

She's really going to make me make the first move, again, isn't she? Fine.

I stub my cig out on the way so I don't turn up all smoky,

and start to cut through the crowd. There is a bit of space to Abs' right, in between her and the mate who helped Kim to give out the drinks earlier, so that's where I aim for. I squeeze through the crowd and as I get close I notice one of the other girls Abs is talking to tap her on the arm and nod in my direction. In turn Abs looks at me and keeps her face plain, playing it cool.

'Alright, you win,' I say to her, grinning wide as I can, 'I can't play it cool any longer. Long time no speak. How are you?'

'Oh, hey, yeah, good thanks,' she says, bit off but I suppose I had brought a lot of energy over. I'll try to tone it back.

'How are you enjoying being back around the old place?'

'Not much has changed. Been a while.'

She isn't giving me much to work with, and I notice her uni mates looking a bit awkward as they give each other side eyes and look into their wine glasses.

'How long have you been back? Saw you away travelling on the socials.'

'You did?'

'Yeah, wasn't it Bali or somewhere like that?'

'How . . . but yeah, Bali and then up through Vietnam and Thailand, yeah.'

'Christ, that's all a bit different from here.'

'Yeah, it was good to celebrate finally finishing up uni.'

'I saw you went in the end. What did you study?'

'Look, I think we're going to head back in, go get a drink.'

'Want me to get you one?'

'It's okay, we're doing rounds and stuff.'

'I'll get the whole round, my treat.'

'Don't worry about it, but thanks.'

'Aight,' I say, and put an arm out to hug her but I barely get an arm on her upper back before she slips away. The fuck was that all about? That was weird. I give them a second thinking I might catch them at the bar and get Abs to change her mind, or at least get a round of shots in to loosen things up a bit, but when I go back I see them hurry into the loos.

I head back downstairs and find Danno and Kim. Looks like they've settled down at a table and were sat next to each other, not too close but thighs touching. I don't see what he sees in her honestly, but it's a sure thing on a night out, I guess. He waves to me to come sit and I point at the bar. We do a bit of mime work and he says he'll take a beer but Kim is good, and so I get drinks and head over. Music has been turned up and the bumble of voices has made it shit-hard to talk. I sit down next to Danno, closer than Kim is to him, and he shouts a thanks for the beer into my ear.

'Where you been at, bruv?' he asks after a sip.

'Went out for a smoke. Chatted to Abs for a bit.'

'You were cool with her, though, yeah? Nothing funny?'

'Nah nah, it was fine. She seemed a bit off.'

'Just leave it for tonight, cuz, yeah?'

Don't know why he's telling me that but I shake it off and have some of my beer.

We have some more drinks and chat some more shit and step outside for a smoke and a bit of air – you know how nights go – and soon an hour or two has passed and I'm back on the dance floor. It's well crowded now and you can't tell where anyone is but we're all just a mass of bodies moving as one, until I see a flick of that red hair in front of me. It's her. Aight, fine, I can get her attention this way. I dance over to her and I put my arm around her shoulder. She whips her head around and her hair swings about my face. It smells of coconut and chocolate and I don't think I've ever liked her more. She clocks us finally and looks confused, it's too loud to hear but I can see her mouth go 'what are you doing?' to me. I want to pull her in to explain that I just want a dance is all, like we used to, and put a hand on her hip to bring her closer so I can lean into her ear but when I do all I get is a push in the chest.

'Fuck off,' I hear, Abs screaming it loud enough to hear over the sound of the club, 'just fuck off and leave me alone, will you?'

She storms off out with her uni mates in tow and I'm confused as fuck. What have I done? Tried to have a chat? Yeah, we got history but I know she's got the rowing fuck and all that, just wanted to have a talk and maybe a dance with an old mate. It's just a dance. Nah, bruv, I'm going to find out what's going on. I make my way out the front to follow her but Danno and Kim are there too.

'The fuck is going on, cuz?' he says to me, and I can tell he's ready.

'Nothing, man. Just asked her for a dance is all, don't know what she's playing at.'

'I told you to be cool, just leave her be.'

'It's just a fuckin' dance, alright, leave it out.'

We're getting hot and Kim is telling us to cool it and soon enough the tall bouncer with shit tattoos is on us saying that we've had enough and need to take it outside. I don't want to – fuck him, I ain't done nothing – but he's a big lad and I don't have a chance against him and now Danno is joining in telling me to just head outside. I can tell Kim is upset and I step towards her to say sorry but Danno grabs me to get me towards the door before the bouncer can get his hands on me.

'Aight, bruv, fuck off, will ya?' I say. Fuck him treating me like a child.

I try and shake him off but on the balance of things I guess he's being a mate. As we get away from the dance floor I start to feel the cool air from the door and, to be honest, yeah, I'm done. Abs has put me in a right shit mood and I just want to get back home. Might see if I can grab the can or two I got at Kim's and I'll go back and watch Netflix or something. But as I'm getting to the street Abs and her friends are just getting their coats from the check girl, and it's my chance to just say sorry, just wanted a dance was all, no hard feelings. I steer my path towards her but now the bouncer don't care if it's Danno on me. I hear the girls shriek as the bouncer takes over and grabs me by the collar and takes me well onto the street. I take a minute to pull my shirt back straight and don't give a shit how big he is any more, I want at him. Danno is on me, though, is pushing me away.

'Come on, bruv, nah, mate, you don't want to do this, let's just get, ya feel me,' he says, while the bouncer is shouting something about getting me out of here. Cunt, making me out to be the bad guy.

I stop fighting Danno and just kind of accept it, turn my back on the club and walk away. I look back and can see Abs and her uni mates going the other way, talking to Kim.

'What did I do?' I yell at them, holding my arms out like I'm on the goddamn cross. 'Just what did I do, yeah?'

'Leave it, be cool, yeah, we gotta get out of here,' Danno says, hand on my chest trying to push me back.

'Nah, nah, just tell me, what did I do?'

I see Abs roll her head back and then start marching my way. Kim and her other mates try to pull her back but she tells them it's okay, and she carries on. The bouncer is looking keen, probably looking for any reason to show off to her by swooping in and saving a day that don't need it, but her uni mate tells him to stand down. Abs stops her march about ten feet away from me and stares at me with her ice blue eyes.

'You treated me like shit when I was too young to know any better,' she says, her voice real steady all of a sudden, 'and I want nothing to do with you. All I wanted was to be able to go out with my best friend on her birthday for the first time in forever, but you couldn't even let me have that.'

I don't know what to say but don't get a chance anyway because Abs has turned and gone off the other way. She stops to say something to Kim and they hug.

'What's she going on about, bruv?' I say to Danno.

'I told you to be cool, just leave it me, man,' he says back.

'What's she saying?' I ask Kim when she walks over to me and Danno.

'I told you to talk to him,' she says to Danno, totally ignoring me.

'I did,' he says, voice high in defence, 'I told him to leave it, yeah.'

'That's it? Just to leave it?'

'Yeah. Just be cool about it.'

'Fucksake,' I say, 'can you not chat like I'm not here, yeah? The fuck is going on?'

'You know why she finally dumped you, yeah?' Kim says to me, squaring up like she was a bloke.

'Shit got bad, we were young, but I'm happy to let bygones be bygones if she just could, yeah? What's her problem?'

'You know why she stuck around that extra year after school, working here?'

'Shit ended bad, guess she needed time.'

'Fucksake, get out of your own arse, alright? She came back to the college to do her law A level so she could go to uni to study it. The exam you told her she was too fuckin' stupid to do, that you convinced her she couldn't hack.'

'You what? I didn't do that shit, man. I wouldn't.'

'You did. Don't matter if you don't realise it or not, fact is you did. And now she's finally back from studying and can come out for – for my fuckin' birthday, Grant, yeah? – but you can't leave her be. She got out of here and is a lawyer now, or nearly one anyway, and that ain't no thanks to you.'

'Nah, you're chatting shit,' I say as I turn on my heel and go. What the fuck was she playing at? Neither of us did that good at school, but the schools around here weren't meant for people like us to do that well in, just in and out and off the street. I never would have told her not to do it, just that it'd be pretty hard.

I stop and light a butt and I hear Danno telling Kim that he'll meet her back at hers. I look over to them and he's jogging back over to me.

'The fuck is she saying, man.'

'You could have just left it, bruv,' he says to me with a sigh and a pant.

'I ain't like that, bruv. I'm not. Why's she even saying that to us?'

'I know you're not.'

'Then why's she saying it?'

'Because, bruv.'

'Because what? You think I'm like that?'

'Nah, cuz, calm it,' Danno says, and I must've been shouting. 'I know you ain't like that and if you were we wouldn't be boys, you get me?'

'Alright, then why's she saying it?'

''Cause to Abs it's how it went down.'

'That's bullshit, bruv. She can just say that, make me out to be the cunt in all this?'

'I ain't looking to dredge it all up.'

'You could've told me.'

'Yeah, and I should have, cuz. That's on me, alright?'

'I didn't do this shit, you all been walking around here thinking I'm the arsehole all these years?'

'Nah, bruv. Just calm down, get some sleep. It'll be calmer tomorrow, fam.'

Fucksake, man. I'm done with him and I turn and head off down the road, both hands deep in my pockets. He shouts something after but I don't got the interest. I ain't like that. I know blokes who are, who treat their boyfriends and girlfriends like utter shit; like maids or like idiots or like cashpoints. I'm not like that. I got a good job – alright, I'm no lawyer, but still – and I treat people well. I've never been like that. Alright, fine, sure, I might not have told Abs to go for it when we were younger but that was the reality of it; we weren't meant for stuff like that. They didn't take people like us anyway, least not then. It's good they do now, she's doing well, but I'm not like that, bruv. I'm not, and I hate people who are. And now, what, people who are my mates have been walking around here for the last five-odd years thinking I am that kinda bloke? Nah, allow it. I'm not. I never have been. I can't be held to blame for maybe one thing I said years ago, it's not like that. I'm not like that. I'm not. I'm not.

Kate

Part One

I knock the front door shut, putting a bookend on the whole situation.

'Well then, what the hell do I do now?' I say out loud to nobody in particular, as there is nobody here to say it to any more.

I look down the short hallway and the kitchen light is still on, and by the sink sits the toast and jam I'd been eating at the time. I take a snort of air to show the scene my displeasure but all it does is tell me that the familiar smell of home didn't seem quite so welcoming any more. I don't know how long I stand with my back pressed up against the front door of our small semi, over the threshold but too weak and, if I'm being honest with myself, too scared to venture further. Time, which had come to a shuddering halt before speeding along at all too much of a disconcerting pace the previous day, has become inconsequential. All I can do is close my eyes to rest myself against the glass in the wooden door and try to breathe, and for a brief moment it feels like pure bliss.

I can feel what's underneath, though, bubbling away and wanting to rage, and I don't even need to recognise it to feel how it wants to make me. I take my breaths real slow and deliberate, almost manual like. I'd read somewhere, or perhaps it was June telling me after reading it in one of her magazines, that breathing slowly calms you down, and how it's something about oxygen helping to process the – oh, what did they call it – the 'panic chemicals' in your brain, wasn't it? Anyway, taking gulps of air and letting more of it pass out your nose – or was it the other way around? – would reduce those kinds of chemicals. Except now I'm not thinking about calming breaths, and the idea of them makes a new association in my brain with June, and thinking about them is the same as remembering us dancing on our silver wedding anniversary or walking down the promenade in Le Touquet hand-in-hand against the biting cold or painting our child's bedroom in anticipation or that night in the West End when it was raining at two o'clock and we couldn't find a taxi for love nor money or how hard it was when we had to turn our child's room back into a study when she didn't make it to her second birthday and, oh, and everything else which a lifetime together brings.

The thought of all of it pushes and I push myself off of the front door, but after only a handful of anxious steps, I find myself halfway down the short hallway. There are gleams of sunlight starting to come through the window in the kitchen and I reckon it must be around seven-thirty, as that was usually the time when the birds started chirping in the trees outside of mine and June's bedroom. My bedroom. The bedroom. Our bedroom. Our old bedroom. Whatever.

I'd left the hospital somewhere around four that morning, perhaps even five, and driven pretty much straight home. On the way the thought had occurred that I should eat something – the first thing people on the telly say is 'When was the last time you've eaten?' – and I'd stopped at an all-night garage to get milk and some bacon, but consciously I couldn't tell you why I'd bothered. Perhaps because my old brain was on autopilot while the higher thinking was shut down through the trauma and exhaustion of it all, and the fact I hadn't eaten for a whole day. Or perhaps I wanted to put some obstacles between where I was and being back at where it had all started. Maybe I'd just wanted to talk to another human being at that hour, sad as it was. Either way, what I bought was sat on the front passenger's seat spoiling under a low, bright sun. Perhaps I just did want to talk to someone, as I know that even if I forced my way back down the hallway towards the front door I couldn't eat what was waiting for me outside through the nausea, just like June on the boats all those years ago.

I'd had my chance to bring it in. When I got home from the hospital I'd sat for the longest time, the radio softly singing me stories about love and sadness, sometimes interrupted by the DJ reading messages out to loved ones who were out on the road somewhere. In a way, the regularity of life made me feel better for a time. It was the same as saying that there were lives out there that were normal, who weren't feeling things from the utter pit, and I couldn't help but take solace in that. Eventually it'd all made me brave enough to step outside into the nose-stinger air, and to come inside. To mine and June's home. To our home. To my home. Whatever.

I storm down the last few feet of the hallway all in a burst and go into the kitchen. Habit tells me to swing around to the left and open the fridge door with the right arm. It's all a bit of an impulse whenever I go through the kitchen, I suppose, but it's double-so when I've got no reason to be digging through it – and I can only remember one day past when I felt like I had this few reasons. Perhaps I am hungry after all. Or, perhaps, I like the idea that through familiarity everything is nice and normal: sat in the fridge door is June's half-eaten pack of lemon slices. I can't understand her love for them, I swear blind that cakes, biscuits, and other such things are supposed to be sweet, not sour. At the thought of her slices I shut the fridge firm enough that I needn't tug on the handle to make sure it had sealed – though I do, of course. If I didn't then I could be sure that June would shout out from her chair to make sure I'd checked it, as one time in 1983 and again in 1997 I had left it ajar and flies had got in. The kitchen is too much and instead I try our small living room, lying heavily on the old, sunken sofa.

I'd thought I was ready for this. Really, I did. I can remember back to sitting in the consultant's drab office, with the walls all faded to a dull grey and furniture which was twenty years out of date. June wasn't scared about the judgement about to be passed down on her; she wasn't naïve to what her body had been saying, and in her mind seeing the doctors was more for a confirmation. In a way, it had been a relief for her when they'd told her.

'Bowel cancer,' the doctor had said, slipping his glasses off in an act I'm sure he'd played a thousand times, 'late stage three, early stage four, without more tests it's hard to tell. I'm sorry.'

He'd let out a well-practised half-smile and maintained eye contact for long enough to seem human before slipping his glasses back on. He pulled out a range of pamphlets he'd already prepared and put them on his desk facing us as he explained what was about to happen. I nodded along dumbly, holding June's hand in her lap while the doctor explained the benefits of each treatment and what the differences between chemotherapy and radiotherapy were. When I looked over at my wife she wasn't quite as receptive to what he was saying.

'I'm sorry to stop you, doctor,' she said with firm control, 'but before we get on to all of this, can't you tell me what it means?'

'I'm not sure I follow you.'

'You've told me I have cancer. I was prepared for it, and don't think I'm scared by it any more, but you've hardly told me I have a cold, have you? I am not going to bounce back from this with a few days in bed and my husband bringing me tea.'

'It's still very early days. It's understandable to be angry or upset, anxious or even numb. It's far too soon to say anything other than we've found it and can start looking into what we can do about it to make sure you have the best quality of life going forward.'

'Please,' she'd said again, firmer this time and with a sharp inhale to steady herself, 'I've never appreciated people skirting the matter at hand. So I'll ask again: what does it mean?'

'It's at a later stage,' the doctor said slowly, again slipping off his glasses, though this time more honestly, 'and if we're being realistic, your age will become a factor. We fight it as aggressively as we can, but statistically the five-year survival rate is under fifty per cent. But that doesn't mean—'

'Thank you,' June said as she stood up, 'we'll be in touch.'

She'd scooped up the leaflets from the table with one hand and pulled me along and out of the door with the other. That'd been twenty-odd months ago now, and it had been nine since my wife had chosen a quality short life over an agonising longer one. I didn't question it when she told me. How could I? I'd lived it with her, why would I wish her to keep going through it.

We both knew that it could happen at any moment, her dying, but in our heads I suppose we'd almost romanticised it. It would play out like some kind of television show or film: she'd be healthy enough until well after the time she was supposed to really get into the trenches with it, and then we'd either get a nurse in or contact one of the hospices the consultant had put us in touch with after she'd refused any more scalpels and needles. Maybe there would be enough time for her sister to come back from Australia, who knew, but in the end she would get to die peacefully like she'd wanted. What I didn't expect was for June to walk down the stairs while I was eating toast, complain of feeling funny, and then collapse in the hallway. I didn't expect our last moments together to be with me pounding away at her chest trying to keep enough blood moving around her body to give her a chance of survival, ignoring the cracks of her ribs as they gave up the ghost, all the while wailing to the voice on the other end of the phone about why a bloody ambulance wasn't here yet. That the last time our lips met would be me desperately blowing air into her lungs. I didn't think that after all of that the process of actually dying would be so complex either, with my June taking the rest of the day and into the early hours of the morning to absolutely and completely leave this world. Even finishing up at the hospital wasn't what I expected it to be. I thought they'd understand, that they'd be there to counsel at least a little bit; a paradox of pain which is universal yet understood to be unique. Instead I stood there in an ammonia-soaked hallway with simply the process of what would happen to my wife's body explained to me by a doctor impatient to get some rest in a staffroom. Eventually, despite my questions, I had to leave or else it would wind up like some kind of awkward first date, with the doctor someone who wasn't too keen about the evening and me unwilling to leave because I was still holding out hope that I'd be invited in.

I think what breaks my heart the most is what is left here. We don't have our child any more, of course, so I don't have a piece of her to still see in that way. June's career had a nice pension but was just secretarial work. It wasn't as if she were a teacher, and had old students coming to drop by the house to talk about their successes and how they'd learned everything they'd needed in her classroom. So what is there? A half-eaten packet of lemon slices in the fridge, and some throw pillows on the sofa which June had loved and I'd thought were pointless because they just got in the way and made the act of sitting harder, but no, she had to have them because they matched the curtains and tied the room together nicely, or something to that effect. Was that all her life was? All our life was? A taste in baked goods and interior design choices? I know what my June was, but to the world . . .

I pick up the picture of us from the side table in my old hands and look at us when we were young. It was from a dinner we'd had in this seaside town in France called Le Touquet, and how we loved going there. By day we'd walk around the shops and the market, stop off in cafés for a coffee or *sixième*, and stroll along the seafront no matter what the wind. At night we'd gorge on fresh-caught seafood and that morning's bread, sometimes talking about what our lives would be when we returned home or sometimes just trying to take in all of the sights and sounds and smells of whichever restaurant we were in. We'd talk about what we'd do with each and every day of our long, happy lives, and of the family we would raise together. Our daughter. And now what? Now you can sum up our accomplishments in baked goods and paint.

I can't take it any more and hug the picture to my chest. I've tried to put it off but I bubble up, and I scrunch my eyes shut tight to try and bargain for a few hours' respite from all of this, but they can't even keep the tears in no more. It passes – though I know it will return – and it is all I can do to lie there.

At some point I must've fallen asleep. It was quite nice waking up, the brief moment of amnesia before I remember why I'm sleeping on the sofa at ten in the morning. First thought I have is it's because I'd been out with some of the old workmates from the plant and come home a little worse for wear, choosing to sleep down here rather than wake June up banging about trying to get me socks off. She always hated it when I'd been out with them; June worked upstairs, me on the floor, and I tried to tease her that she'd become an upstairs person but it did not go well. Might be why I never kept in touch with any of the guys when we retired, and what with June getting ill so soon after I didn't exactly have the time to reconnect.

It doesn't hurt at the moment. Maybe this is like when a boxer breaks his hand: it hurts like all hell at the time, and it'll hurt again afterwards, but your brain numbs it for the moment so that you can carry on the fight. Looks like there are no excuses left: I've got to call June's sister. June had gone around four this morning, and I'd like to think I would be within six hours if any of my family died. Theoretically, at least. It'll still be about seven o'clock in Australia. I drag myself off the sofa and go into the kitchen, picking up the landline and starting the long process of calling Australia. I know you can do it on your mobile or the internet these days but I don't know how to do any of that and don't really have anyone to show me, so I still do it the way we always did: dial into the account that offers the cheap international calls, dial in the PIN, tell it where you want to call, punch in the number you wanted to get through to all along, and then wait to see if the system will work or if you'll have to start over again. While I'm waiting I use my elbow to nudge open the kitchen cupboard near the back door and pop out the pack of cigarettes which June knows I keep there but decides not to say anything about. I open the back door while the phone does its holding pattern and step out into the world. It's still as cold as it was this morning, but in the places where the sunlight snuck through it seemed like the warmth was making progress. I light and exhale as the dial tone goes through its final transformations.

'Yes? Hello?' Sylvia says tersely as she answers.

'Uh, hi, Sylvia. It's Martin,' I reply, offering little in retaliation for once.

'Oh, shit, I'm sorry. We just sat down for dinner here and I thought it would be somebody asking about a car crash we didn't have.' Her accent was still clearly from around here, but had picked up a little bit of an Australian twang. Didn't surprise me; it'd been, what, twenty-five years now? Had both of her kids there, and they were at uni by now. They might've even graduated. I'm not sure, June is in charge of sending cards and such things. Was in charge. Used to be. Whatever.

'Yeah, I'm sorry to bother you at this time, it's just that . . .' and I lose my voice. I know I should be telling her, quickly but firmly, what was going on over on this side of the world, but all of a sudden I've got no idea how I'm going to. And, I don't want to. Admitting it to Sylvia would mean admitting it was real. Talking about it means it has happened. My wife has died. June has died.

'You're calling me at – what – ten in the morning your time, Martin,' Sylvia says with a sigh that sounded like resignation, 'something's happened, hasn't it?'

'Yes.'

'Well, what?'

I had to blurt it out in the end: 'June died this morning, Sylvia. I'm sorry.'

'Died? What do you mean died?' Sylvia seemed to stumble for words for a moment before continuing. 'How could you let this happen?' she spat with a kind of venom far worse than when we fought before.

'What do you mean how could I let this happen? She was ill, I didn't do anything. It just happened!'

'She was supposed to have until at least the summer so I could visit.'

'There was nothing I could do!' I say to her but the words get no weight behind them.

'You could have cared more.'

'How could I?'

'She was never the same after what happened. Never. In a way you . . .' and Sylvia stopped talking mid-sentence, though I'm well aware of what the end of it was going to be. She's said it before, drunk, on the anniversary. I'm sure I can hear a clatter as she whips the phone away from her mouth before she says it again. Real faint from the background I can hear her family asking what was wrong, perhaps a sob or two as well.

'Look, when is the funeral going to be?' she eventually asks.

'Should be a week, maybe ten days tops. We made a lot of plans beforehand.'

'Well, we'll see about them. Look, I've got to go. I need to look about flights and seeing what I'll do with work. I'll let you know when I'm going to get in the country.'

'Do you want me to get the spare room ready here? Pick you up from the airport?'

'No, I'll get a hotel and email when I'm here. Then we can plan for the funeral.'

'June and I have everything she wanted planned out, pretty much. I just need to make some calls and book things. If you need a few more days to get out here, I can take care of it.'

'She is my sister, too,' Sylvia snaps at me. 'I get a say in how to say goodbye to her.'

'Okay.'

'I need to go. I'll let you know when I'm in the country.'

With that she hung up on me. I drop the cigarette butt to the floor and kick it into the flower bed so that June won't see it, and don't know whether to laugh or cry at the thought. I go back inside, put the phone back in the cradle and look down our hall towards the front door. The post has been delivered while I've been gone, an electric bill for me and one of June's lifestyle magazines for her. I'll have to look into how to cancel those, I guess. I look at the clock in the kitchen and it is 10.14 a.m. on a Tuesday.

'What do I do now?' I say out loud again, still holding out hope for an answer that will never come again.

Part Two

June had driven from our new house to the port at Dover and I was going to drive from Calais to Le Touquet. She'd never liked driving on the 'wrong' side of the road and always got seasick whenever she was on the ferry, and so appreciated being able to sit quietly in the car for the final hour or so of the journey. After the first time we'd taken the ferry over she'd almost wanted to make it a one-time thing, dreading the seasickness that accompanied it and thinking about the feasibility of flying back home when the trip was done. It had been our first proper holiday abroad together, and the first time she'd been on a ferry. Once the nausea wore off, though, she'd had the time of her life – we both did – so much so that she didn't mind feeling worse for wear on the way back. She saw the doctors to find ways of fending off the seasickness and ferries became a regular fixture in the years following.

We managed to coincide one such pilgrimage with our eighth wedding anniversary. It had been eleven since that first trip and, though we'd started venturing further afield, this time we weren't visiting anywhere else: we were spending the whole week in Le Touquet. It was a week for staying up late as we drank strong coffees with large glasses of calvados in trendy cafés. We would get up early and go for brisk morning walks along the beach to blast out the previous night's decadence, and then go back to bed around eleven to work up the appetite for lunch. We would be us, to the fullest we could be.

'What do you want to do first?' June asked as we got close to the town. I'd let her sit quietly, and June asking a question like that was her way of saying that the ferry's ill effects had worn off.

'Well, I can think of one thing,' I said back. We were young, then.

'Okay,' said June, giggling like she did, 'after that. It's still quite early. What will you want to do?'

'Walk around town a bit, see what's changed, see if there are any new restaurants or shops opened up. Go for a drink. We should buy a paper, too, and see if it's going to be warm enough to do much at the beach this year, perhaps.'

'Maybe have a look to see what properties have come on the market.'

'We just bought a house, and it was a nightmare. You want to do it again?'

'I'm sure Quarry Lane will be lovely, but can't I dream of a place here, too?'

I remember smiling to myself as I changed lanes to get ready for pulling off the motorway and onto the smaller roads which led to the town's centre.

'You deserve one, but you know we can't afford to buy anywhere here, even if we were to rent it out for the fifty-odd weeks a year when we're not using it.'

'I know, it's just nice to see what the market is doing. You never know if prices are going to go down a bit, or if there is somewhere for sale on the cheap, or something.'

I said nothing but glanced away from the road to give her a look.

'Shut up, it could.'

We spent most of that afternoon enjoying our room: the view, the balcony, and the four-poster bed. That night we held hands as we wandered into town to go to one of our favourite seafood restaurants and ordered a *plateau de fruits de mer royale* and a bottle of Chablis – and then another – as we spent hours picking our way through the extravagant tower of oysters, crab, lobster, langoustine, prawns, brown shrimp, whelks, and winkles, laughing and joking as we drank, not least at the word 'winkle', which we found as funny then as we did the first time we'd eaten them. The waiter took our picture when we handed him our camera, and when we were home we framed it and put it on the side to remind ourselves of that night. After dinner we headed to a nearby café and drank espresso along with two large glasses of brandy each, then headed to bed once again. It didn't feel like a celebration of eight years of marriage, it was like we were simply continuing on from our first trip there.

The next morning brought more of the same. I bought some new shirts from one of the designer outlets along with a rustic desk lamp made out of driftwood at the market, while June found herself a new summer coat and hat combination. We had lunch near the seafront – I remember having *moules frites* and June chose a *croque-monsieur* – before we lingered outside of a children's clothes shop as we walked back towards our hotel. As the sun began to dip in the sky we decided to go for a long walk along the seafront to build up our appetite before going out for a *pierade*. We had to wrap up more than the time of year should have called for to fend off the stiff breeze coming in from the Channel. The walkway by the beach was elevated above the sand and reeds, and we had a clear view of families flying kites as the sun set.

'So, I'm going to say a word now,' said June as we walked hand in hand, 'and I don't want you to overreact or anything. I just want to see what your thoughts are.'

'If it's brandy then I agree, let's wait until later, after last night I'm still feeling a little jaded.'

'Martin, can you please be serious about this? Just for a little bit?'

'That may be a struggle.'

'Try?'

'Perhaps.'

A tug on my hand made me realise that June had stopped walking. She was wearing one of those faces that told me this was most definitely not a joking matter, and that being serious was non-negotiable. I pulled her close and planted a kiss on her forehead before we carried on walking, albeit slower now, as if walking were secondary and we were merely drifting in the wind together, floating to where the world wanted to take us.

'Children,' June blurted out.

'Children?'

'Children. It's just I love you so much, and I've loved the last eight years of our lives, and everything. We've got good jobs at the plant, we've got the new house, so we can support a family. And, plus, you know.'

'Know what?'

'Well, I'm not as young as I used to be. And Mum hit the menopause early so who knows how many years I've got left to have children before it's too late. And I don't think there is a version of our life where I wouldn't want to have them with you at some point.'

'So you want children, plural?'

'Perhaps.'

I stopped our drifting and pulled June around to face me. I could see the worry etched into her face and tried to ease it with a gentle smile.

'So, tell me about the children we're going to have,' I said to her, not brave enough to tell her an outright 'yes'. Saying it would mean accepting it as fact, and although I too had been thinking about the notion of children, it would take me more than a few seconds to get my head around it becoming a fully verified plan.

'I figured a girl, perhaps, and if all goes well then another one. And a little brother for them to torment, too.'

'You've really thought about this.'

'Of course, but this isn't just me. This will change both of our lives forever. Just because I'm at the stage where this is what I want, it doesn't mean that you have to be ready to start a family. This won't change how much I love you.'

I kissed her to tell her that I agreed, that we were ready. I loved her, maybe more in that moment than ever, and wanted nothing else than to start a family with her, to fill our new house with even more affection, even if I couldn't say it out loud yet. June was right: we'd had eight wonderful years as a married couple, and our lives looked so promising. Maybe it was time.

'So, tell me about this daughter we're going to have,' I said as I again took June's hand. We carried on our slow amble, but this time towards the town and the small restaurant by the dock whose patio was protected from the wind with a giant perspex screen and where waiters brought you hot stones to cook your own selections of meat and seafood on.

'Well,' started June as she took advantage of our slower pace, leaning her head on my shoulder as the white streetlights began to glow overhead, 'I figure she'll start out as a bit of a tomboy before blossoming into a princess. She'll grow up to be beautiful and talented and successful and will take care of us in our old age, because no matter how much I love you I think we'll need some distraction when you're too blind to read the smaller bits of the newspaper and I'm too deaf to hear you ask what the words are. Plus grandkids would be nice when we're at that stage, I hear they keep you young.'

'You've thought of everything else. Do you have a name in mind for this young lady who'll keep us from going mad when we grow old?'

'Kate.'

Tea

'Ah, fuck, Katie,' moans Stephen as he grips onto me, left hand on my shoulder and right on my hip. He starts thrusting deeper and harder, and I arch my back to help meet his strokes. With my right hand I pull my panties aside and start kneading the head of my cock; he won't do it for me. He'll sometimes reach out, tentative like, and run his fingers over it, but he's more interested in using me.

Not that I entirely hate that, or else I wouldn't spend my Friday evenings dressing myself, waiting for him to come over.

Stephen's pace picks up again and he's almost lifting me off the bed as he slides himself in and out of me. I close my eyes and bury my face into the bed, wrapping my silk-glove-covered hand around my cock and tugging it with tight, quick pumps. I tuck the long blonde locks from my wig behind my ears and grind my face into the clean sheets I'd put on the bed for that night; I know he loves the muffled groans and it gives me a strong enough base to stop him fucking me clean off the bed.

His pace slows up, and he says something. I don't hear what he says, too caught up in the moment.

'What?' I ask, trying hard to keep my voice feminine enough for him.

'Your wig,' he says gruffly.

'What about it?'

'Put your fucking wig back on,' he shouts, leaning forward and jabbing the palm of his hand into the front of my ribs. My body tenses up on impact, and he lets out a moan as he enjoys the feeling of it while inside of me.

'Your fucking wig,' he says again, me not fixing it quick enough for his liking. This time he closes his fist and hits me in the same place, not like a punch but more like swinging a club. It makes me grunt, and not in a good way.

'Sorry,' I mumble as I pull the long blonde wig back into place, covering up my natural short black hair. I'd had it cut shorter than normal, and the hair clips must be struggling for traction to hold Katie's hair on.

Hair fixed, Stephen starts on me again, both hands on my hips and aggressive. It hurts a bit, but by far not the worst I've had, and I start working on myself to try to get into it.

'That's right, baby, fuck me hard,' I say, trying to help him get back into the moment.

He tells me to shut up.

'I'm not going to be able to cum like this now,' he says eventually, pulling out and rolling the condom off in one fluid movement. I sit up, slipping my cock back into my panties to make sure that he won't have to see it, and watch him as he lays down on the bed, parting his legs. I know what he wants and get to work.

I let out soft moans and look up at Stephen, trying to give him the full effect of the eye make-up I'd spent an age doing, but he has his eyes closed. Eventually he starts to run his hand through my hair, and I stop rubbing myself to hold on to the wig so it doesn't slip off again. I put my hand on top of Stephen's to try to control the pace with which he's bobbing my head up and down. It's not too fast, but his wedding ring is clunking off my skull each time he does it.

As he finishes he lets out a loud gasp and holds my head in place, expecting me to swallow it all. I manage most of it. Stephen takes a minute to recover before getting dressed quickly; he never hangs about afterwards. I lay on the bed while he puts his suit trousers and shirt back on. He likes the idea that I'm used up and it's all I can do to just lie there. His shirt is a bit tight and the soft edges of his muscles make him look more built than he really is, and his deep caramel skin really stands out against the white cotton. It's hot as fuck.

'See you next week, sexy,' he says as he sees himself out. Soon as I hear the doors shut I begin to undress; wig brushed and back on the stand, silk gloves and panties into their own basket so I can hand-wash them later, padded bra into the regular wash, torn tights into the bin. I take a shower to wash the sweat, make-up, cum, and lube off of me. I finish myself off there too after not being given the chance to do so when Stephen was here. I think about the second or third time he'd been over. We met dogging, he seemed safe and liked what I did to his cock. He'd started coming around. It's usually from behind, not doing anything to me but fucking me, but one time he'd flipped me over so I could ride him. He'd reached out and stroked me too, letting me cum all over his smooth chest. Only time he'd done it. Still cum hard to that thought. Doesn't compare to what it would have felt like to climax with him fucking me tonight, but it's still pretty powerful after being on edge for so long. I have to grab onto the shower fittings to stop my legs from giving way.

I dry off and go to the kitchen in just some pyjama bottoms to make a cup of tea. My mobile starts ringing while I'm waiting on the kettle. It's Kevin, one of the lads I dress up and go clubbing with.

'Y'alright, mate?' I say as I answer the phone, pinning it between my ear and shoulder as I root through the cupboard for sugar.

'Not bad, Gareth, not bad,' he says, 'didn't catch you at a bad time, did I? Haven't still got your Friday Fella there?'

'No, he just left, and so here I am, alone again,' I say with suitable melodrama.

'No plans with him for tomorrow?'

'There's a reason we call him the Friday Fella.'

'Well, then, if you fancy it,' Kevin says, letting out a low-pitched laugh, 'few of us are heading into central for the Glitter Girls night. Got a good deal on a hotel room up there, were going to have some drinks there, get dressed, head out. Fancy it?'

'Yeah, sounds like fun. I might come already dressed.'

'Yeah, we know about you; lucky bastard who can pass pretty easily. I try that and I get the looks that remind me I'm a brickie in a dress.'

'You shut up,' I say to him. Kevin's always getting himself down and worrying about passing rather than enjoying himself, 'you look great. I'll come by early, help you get ready.'

'Thanks, mate, I'd appreciate it. You looking to stay there too?'

'Nah, I've got work on Sunday. I'll head home.'

'Yeah, yeah, work, whatever. You're just certain you'll pull.'

'I can't possibly begin to think what you might be on about.'

We finish chatting and I re-boil the kettle. I throw the sheets in the wash while it bubbles away too, and put my regular ones back on the bed, but there's still a faint smell of sex and perfume in the room.

I get dressed as Katie and walk to the train station: blonde wig again, this time with a little black dress and heels. Cover it all up with a long beige coat with fur around the neck. The only dodgy bit is walking out of the Quarry, never know what reaction I'll get here, but once I'm on the train I enjoy the looks. London loves me.

The hotel is one of the chain ones near Leicester Square; looks nice but everything is wipe-clean. I find the others in the room and promptly get presented with a glass of prosecco. There are two others up there along with Kevin, and they tell me their names but I quickly forget them. Seem nice enough though; one is dressed and the other one doesn't. As promised I help Kevin get ready, though it isn't easy, and he looks quite good in the end. It takes an inch of foundation to hide the fact that his stubble grows back within a half-hour of shaving, and nothing will disguise his broad shoulders, but he looks better than normal. Makes me glad that I'm twenty-two going on fifteen; I've always been scrawny, and it's easy to make boyishness look feminine.

'Tonight,' Kevin declares, 'I'm going to be Electra,' he says, elongating the last syllable and fluttering his eyes to draw attention to the vivid blue shadow around them. He changes his persona every time, rarely the same person twice. I'm always Katie; she's a big part of me.

'Thank you, Gar— I'm sorry, excuse me, Katie,' Electra says to me. I smile as she starts tearing up.

'Don't you worry, and don't you bloody start crying. I'm not doing your sodding eyes again.'

'I know how to cure that,' Electra says, reaching for an unopened bottle of prosecco and easily popping the cork out with a single strong hand.

The four of us finish off three bottles between us before we head out. Not enough to get drunk, but it's a nice buzz. The club is a five-minute walk away and the street is full of the usual crowd; some dressed as full-on, flamboyant drag queens, some trans, others who dress for fun, all rounded out by big groups of regular guys and admirers. Despite the streets being full of friendly faces, Electra is still nervous. She's had some trouble before – something about being dressed does it to people, because when she's not dressed Kevin is the kind of bloke you'd go out your way to not get into a ruck with – and I hold her hand. She gives it a squeeze.

It's still early when we get there, barely half ten, but the line is already starting to snake. We get in the back and light cigarettes, giggling about whatever comes up. There's a group of guys in front of us, most of them making sly eyeballs like a bunch of schoolboys not knowing how to react when the Year 11 girl with big tits gets on the bus. They're mostly a bunch of middle-aged blokes, shirts which probably fit last year being tested by pudgy mid-sections, but there's one who looks good there. He's a bit younger, and fit; not big, but toned like a runner. Rather than shooting awkward sideways glances, he looks at me dead on and smiles. I smile back, knowing how to work my face and raise my left cheek to give a flirty smirk.

The line moves quick and it only takes us fifteen minutes to get inside. It's already busy and I'm glad we got here earlier than usual, they'll go to one-in-one-out soon. Hotel-room scene will be good tonight, though, load of people dressed and ready with no place to go. The others make a beeline to the bar but I don't, it's twenty quid for a watered-down drink and I've got work in the morning anyway. I drop my coat off in the room and head to the loo. I wait for a stall, but only to get the baggie with an E in it out from the front of my knickers. I pop it in and get a mouthful of water from the tap. The others have found a bit of ledge by the dance floor and Electra has bought me a G&T anyway as a thank you.

We finish up and they get another round before we dance. The tab kicks in and the hours pass. At some point I stop dancing with my group and the guy from the line finds me. He says something in my ear but it's too loud to hear. Instead I reply by moving my body against his, and I feel his hands grip onto my hips. Every now and then between kisses he moves a hand slightly forwards, brushing his fingers against the side of my cock gently in contrast to how hard he's controlling my body with his other. I'm soon telling Electra that I'm getting my coat.

Outside in the quiet he tells me his name is Samuel, and I tell him my only rules are that we go to my place and he doesn't sleep over. He agrees and we walk beneath the West End's neon glow, loosely holding hands, towards a night bus. He tells me sweet things, or it could be anything with the tab still running through me, and I can't wait to get him back. He looks like he can go for hours. We get on the night bus and spend the forty minutes it takes to get out of central stealing little kisses from each other. As the bus quietens down I start to rub his cock through his jeans. We stop when the bus does, and I have to put my bag over my lap to hide my erection from people shuttling through the aisle.

We get off in the heart of the Quarry and walk down the high street towards my flat. It's late, past two, and the streets are dead. Pubs have long since kicked out and the local club is way on the other side of town. We walk quicker, bored of travelling and eager to get to the next stage, but I get a hot sweat of nerves when I see a car drive by us. I know it well, a Mercedes SLK which is often parked outside my flat.

'Shit,' I say, sounding more like me and less like Katie, 'can we duck in here?' I try to pull Samuel down an alley to hide but he roots himself, and all that happens is me swinging back into him.

'What's wrong? We're nearly back at yours, you said,' he says, being all kind but he doesn't know.

Down the street the SLK has done a U-turn and come back towards us, stopping with two wheels up on the pavement and hazards on. I try to shepherd Samuel down one of the side streets again but again he's stubborn, not sure what's going on. I want to tell him to just go along with it, that we're going back and I'll fuck him anyway, not to worry about all of this, yes, I know it's weird but trust me. I don't get the chance, and it's too late anyway.

'What's this then, eh?' comes a shout from down the street from Stephen.

'Just leave it out, yeah,' I say to Stephen, not working to keep my voice real feminine.

'Leave it out? Fuck off. Who's this then?' he shouts, striding up to Samuel and me. He looks like he's dressed up for the night, tight white shirt that show off his muscles, and jeans. He's pissed as hell, but looks great. Fucker.

'No one, just leave us alone,' I say, but Stephen has pushed past me already.

'Yeah, yeah, who the fuck are you?' he says to Samuel, getting into his face.

'Easy, leave it out, yeah,' Samuel says, but as he tries to back off things but Stephen just keeps pushing forward.

'Alright, that's enough,' I say and try to get myself between them. I push into Stephen's firm chest and he lets me shepherd him back a bit towards the shutters on the Paddy Power. Samuel starts after us, mouth gawping but I tell him to stay put and he does. He takes to pacing on the spot, looking like he wants to run but holding out for chivalry, or hoping he can still get a fuck, or some other selfish bullshit.

'What are you doing?' I say to Stephen, trying hard to sound reasonable.

'What am I doing? The fuck are you doing? Taking some random cock home to suck on?'

'Just leave it out, will you? Go home, or wherever it is you were off to.'

'I was on my way around to yours. Thought we could have another go. Why are you going around looking for someone else, huh?'

Stephen keeps shooting daggers over my shoulder at Samuel.

'It's Saturday night,' I say, 'what are you on about? You think I sit at home all week waiting for the off-chance you want to come back over?'

'Bitch,' he snarls at me.

'Oh, fuck off,' I say, 'and what were you doing out at this time? Didn't find anyone in a wig dogging at Wisley so now you're on a slow, sad drive home?'

He gives me a right hard shove and I can't catch the balance in my heels, slipping straight on my arse and jamming my palms into the pavement.

'The fuck are you doing? Leave her alone,' Samuel shouts at Stephen, finding a pair out of nowhere and charging at him.

Stephen meets his charge and spins Samuel around, banging him against the shutters and setting off an almighty racket. Stephen tries punching Samuel in the ribs but they've got ahold of each other and he can't get his arm back to land anything with any power. The heel has come off my left shoe where Stephen shoved me and my beige coat is torn and stained from where I slid along the wet pavement.

'Stop it, will you?' I shout at the two men as they bounce each other off the shutters. A few lights in the flats above the shops have turned on, and I can see heads peeking out. I open up my handbag and pull my phone out, but don't know what I'm going to do with it. Do you call the police because some guy who comes around to fuck you is having a fight with some random fella you brought home from the club? What if the police call me 'miss' and then ask to take my name?

Stephen breaks Samuel's grip and steps back. Samuel gets one swing away and lands an awkward left hook onto Stephen's right temple, and I can see it's opened up a nick across his eyebrow. Samuel doesn't follow it up, though, doesn't know what Stephen's like, and thinks that a little cut will scare him off. Of course it doesn't, and Stephen flies back. He swings two big rights at Samuel's head, and Samuel puts his arms up like chicken wings to protect himself. He's not a fighter and leaves his ribs open, and Stephen throws two big hits there, too, leaving Samuel in a ball on the ground. Stephen goes to walk away before doubling back and giving Samuel a big kick in the gut for good measure.

'I swear, Stephen,' I say to him, still sat in a puddle and fumbling with the passcode on my phone, 'I swear. I'll call the police. I will.'

'Don't you fucking dare,' he growls at me. I stop, and he squats down in front of me. Behind him I can hear Samuel coughing up something wet and bad.

'No more fucking around,' Stephen says to me, right in my face, 'you hear me?'

I nod, and he reaches a hand out to my face. Makes me flinch, but instead he just brushes some of the hair away and runs his thumb over my cheek.

'I'll see you Friday,' he says before standing up.

From somewhere around the corner a police siren kicks off and Stephen looks up real quick. He jogs back to his still-running car and guns it off down the high street, back of the car squealing and squirming from the power and slick road.

The sirens were off to somewhere else in the Quarry – can tell Stephen doesn't live around here, thinking he was the only one doing something that the coppers would be interested in – and it was just me and Samuel left. I stand up shaking and go over to him. He's got a massive welt around his eye and thick, blood-stained mucus dribbling out of his mouth. He looks at me, half pissed off and half like a puppy. I dial 999 and tell them that a guy had the shit kicked out of him in front of the Paddy Power on Quarry Lane, and he's got some blood coming up from inside. That'll put him to the top of the list, internal bleeding gets you bumped up above the broken ankles to just below the heart attacks. They tell me they've already had a few calls to get police to that area.

'I'm sorry,' I say to him, but his eyes have glazed over, 'they won't be long. Police are coming too, I can't stay. I'm sorry.'

I take my shoes off and start to jog down the high street but stop when I see blue flashing lights at the corner; I'm trying to avoid looking like I know anything about the guy coughing up blood down the street. Running away isn't a good look. I'm barely fifty metres away when the police speed past me. I keep my head down, but after one officer jumps out to look after Samuel the blues-and-twos go back on and the car comes back down the street in the high whine of reverse.

'Sorry, miss,' says a female officer, jumping out of the driver's seat, 'can you stop, we need to have a word.'

'Oh, let me tell you, it was awful,' I say to Janine at work, having a cuppa before browsing time ended at John Lewis and we had to get onto the shop floor. I was careful as I drank, not wanting an errant drip of tea to find its way onto my freshly ironed white shirt or green tie.

'Bloody hell, Gareth, what a 'mare,' Janine says, blowing out smoke from a rollie. I shift slightly to make sure I stay upwind, not wanting to spend the day smelling like an ashtray.

'What are you going to do?'

'Don't know, see if the guy does anything about it and wait for a letter through the door, I guess,' I say. She liked to hear about my weekends and I'd told her about the scrap, ambulance and all. I'd skipped over the fact I was dressed. Completely left out the look on the officer's face when she realised I was.

'I mean, what are you going to do about the old Friday Fella you go on about?'

'No idea. Don't want to text him. Police said I shouldn't. See if he shows up, I guess.'

'What if he shows up, though? All angry or something? You going to be alright? I could have a word with Prescott, see if he could come over that night or something.'

'That's kind, but it'll be alright. Got all week to figure it out.'

The boss sticks his head out back and says the floor is opening. Janine steps on her cig and we head in. She's in Home, I'm upstairs in White Goods. Not a bad job, get a bit of commission on the big stuff. Ovens, fridges, dishwashers, that kind of thing. It's a typical Sunday morning, a lot of browsers. People these days see something they want, then get the phones out to see if it's cheaper online. I go up, do the niceties, ask if they need anything, and they all try to hide the fact they've got Amazon open.

There's one woman, though, taking a good look at a fancy stove in a mock-up kitchen as she tries to deal with a baby in a pram. Thing she's looking at is bloody massive: half-dozen hobs, two ovens, all magnetic controls, and costs more than everything in my flat twice over. Nice, though, if you can afford it. I make a beeline over to her and see Derek, the other guy on the floor with me, throw a quick scowl out. He's stuck with a studenty-looking couple fussing about a cheapo microwave. When I get over she's got her head stuck in the stroller, trying to win silence via cooing noises. It's a nice stroller, a Bugaboo; she can afford the oven.

'Beautiful, isn't it?' I say to her. She pops her head out and looks at the oven.

'Yeah, and then some,' she says.

'I meant your little one,' I say, camp as I can. Housewives love that, so I play it up. They think that membership to the queer club gives me superior interior design insight. She laughs and I put my hand on her arm. She's dressed in black riding boots, tight jeans, and has got a leather jacket on with an unnecessarily fluffy collar. It looks like she crashed through the front door of River Island.

'The oven's nice as well, though,' I say, 'is this the sort of thing you're looking for?'

'Something like this, yeah. Having the kitchen re-done. Proper nightmare. Knocking down the back wall, bit of an extension, normal-sized thing's gonna look right stupid in it now, y'know?'

'So you're after a stove which is a centrepiece for the room?'

'Yeah, something like that. It's nice to hang out in the kitchen when people are over, cook a nice meal and stuff. The husband wanted us to get an Aga, told him to forget it. Not learning how to cook on one of those things.'

I give her the sales spiel: features, guarantee, delivery, how you have to get the special magnetic pots to use with it, but we've got a good deal on them. She cooed at that bit, taking mental notes on how to show it off when people are over.

'I'll have to find my husband,' she says, rocking the pram gently after the little one lets out a few squeaks, 'he's off somewhere looking at the tellies. Take him anywhere and he goes off towards the shiny things.'

We both laugh and she spots him over my shoulder, waving him over. I straighten up the brochure, getting ready for the hard sell. Wives love the gay man act, but husbands think it makes them stronger so they can beat me down on price a bit.

'Here y'are, love,' she says to him. I turn around and I'm face to face with him. With *him*.

'This is who was helping me,' she carries on, 'and look at this thing. This is . . .' She trails off.

'Gareth,' I say to her with a smile, shaking her lightly by the hand. 'And it's still Gareth,' I say to him, firm but friendly, and extend my hand. When his reaches mine I can see his red knuckles.

'Stephen,' he says, doing a quick shake before snatching his hand away. He has a nick above his eye from where Samuel lamped him one. He didn't get it stitched and it's like a small, squashed raspberry on his eyebrow.

'Well, I was just explaining to your lovely wife here . . .' and I trail off when I try to do her name.

'Caroline,' she says with a giggle, 'we're bad at names here, aren't we?'

'As I was just telling Caroline here, if you're looking for a real centrepiece for your new kitchen, this stove can be it.'

'I don't know,' he says, looking at Caroline, 'this is big. Maybe we should keep looking, go somewhere else. Might have something better. No offence meant, mate,' he says, looking at me.

'Of course, none taken,' I say back to him, big smile on my face, 'there are a lot of options out there. But this is a great model, and buying from us will give you the best value.'

'Still, I think we should look at an Aga. It'll fit the room, plus you get free cooking courses when you buy one.'

'I don't want an Aga,' Caroline says, 'I love this one. It's well smart. Uses magnets and everything.'

'The problem with an Aga,' I say, 'is that they're not very economical unless you cook daily. You could just use this once a week and get away with it,' I say to Stephen. I watch his face twitch, wanting to lash out, but knowing he can't. I can see why he likes having the power; it feels nice.

The baby chirps up again, this time with a proper whimper, and Caroline bends down to deal with it. Stephen looks at me, not angry or mean like, but rattled. He looks tired; clothes are different from last night, but he doesn't look like he's slept.

'You have a stinky bottom,' Caroline says to the sobbing baby, 'yes you do, yes you do, you have a stinky bottom. I'm going to go and change him, can you sort this out, love?'

'I don't know about it,' Stephen says again, 'it's kind of plain, just a bit of a gimmick. Maybe we should look for something better.'

'I spend all the time in that house, not you,' she says with a bit of venom, 'this is perfect. I'm going to go and change him, you sort this out.'

Caroline picks the baby bag up from the bottom of the stroller and turns to me.

'He might look like a thug with his new eyebrow scar, but he's alright really. Won't hurt ya. Out late roughhousing with his mates. They drink red wine and vodka to get each other all messed up, can you believe it! Silly sod fell down, didn't he?'

Stephen smiles, playing his part well. I don't think he's fooling his wife, though, who leans in towards his ear.

'Look, you,' she says in a harsh whisper, but loud enough for me to hear, 'this is what I want. And this is a nice man, don't be cruel to him. Just order the kitchen, none of your usual nonsense, alright?'

Stephen nods. He smiles at her but down by his side I can see a fist clenching and unclenching.

'Play nice,' she says to him, looking friendly for my benefit, as she takes the baby away. We're left alone, me in a suit and him with a cut and assault charge hanging over him.

'So, should we—' I ask before he cuts me off.

'Fine. What she says, I'm sure you heard. Do whatever.'

'It costs—'

'That's fine.'

'Okay.'

'Okay.'

'We'll need a fridge too,' he says, 'big one.'

'This range has one,' I say, 'matches. Double doors. Deep freezer doors. Water filter and ice built in, American-style. It's—'

'That's fine.'

'It'll cost—'

'That's fine too.'

'And the stove needs magnetic pans, which—'

'Just add it on.'

'Okay.'

'Okay.'

We stand there, both looking down at the brochure. Would think we were discussing the finer points of oven ownership if you looked at us.

'Did you know him?' Stephen asks quietly.

'Know him?'

'Like, was he, you know . . .'

'I met him that night.'

'I'm sorry,' he says, even quieter.

'Sorry?'

'Yeah. I'm sorry.'

'Don't have anything to do with me,' I say. 'I was just there.'

'Is he going to do anything about it?' Stephen asks.

'Police pick you up?'

'Yeah. Got to go back on Friday.'

'It's not for me to do anything about, is it?'

'You could talk to him.'

'I don't know him. Not a number. Don't even know how he is.'

'He spent the night in, they said.'

We make busy work of staring at the black granite countertop.

'Police said I shouldn't talk to you,' Stephen says, barely above a whisper.

'Everything says I shouldn't talk to you,' I say back, before carrying on with, 'I should write all this up.'

'All what up?'

'The stove. Fridge. Pans.'

'Okay.'

We go over to one of the counters and I start building the invoice. It's about four and a half grand, all in.

'Last name?' I have to ask. It's been about six months I've been fucking him and I haven't had cause to know it until now.

'Russell. It's Russell. Two Ls,' he says, looking over my shoulder towards the direction his wife went.

'Home number?'

'Why do you need that?' he asks, eyes all narrow.

'Just for delivery. Don't worry.'

'We don't have one,' he says to his shoes after a pause, 'we just use mobiles. Mine's—'

'Don't worry,' I say, typing, 'I know it. Address?'

Stephen rubs the balls of his hands into his eyes, gently brushing at his fresh scar with his fingertips.

'I need your address,' I say again.

'Isn't there someone else who I can do this with?' Stephen asks.

'It's a commission sale.'

'How much? I'll just pay you,' he says, getting his wallet out and bouncing it on the counter. There's a sea of purple and red sticking out of the top.

'It goes on my sales quota for the month, all of that. I just need your address.'

He tells me. I know where it is, few miles away from the Quarry, full of big back gardens and German cars. I run his credit card and it clears no problem.

'All sorted?' Caroline asks, back from the changing rooms with a decidedly happier baby.

'Of course, love, all sorted,' he says, planting a small kiss on the top of her head.

'You're good to me,' she says, and plants a short kiss on his lips before tucking the baby back in the stroller. I give them the delivery details, and the number they can call to sort out installation and all of that. She takes the card and puts it in her purse.

'Lunch?' she says to him as she tucks it back in her

handbag. 'Or can you not face being in a pub again this soon?'

'I think I could go for a pint and a roast.'

They line up to say their thanks to me. Caroline goes first and gives me a little squeeze before turning to push the stroller away. Stephen goes next, but it's just a quick handshake and he doesn't say anything.

I go the rest of the week without shaving, letting a patchy moustache and little tuft on my chin try to have their day. The section manager at work gives me stick about it, says it looks untidy, and I tell him it'll either be filled out or gone when I'm back on Sunday.

I don't go out Thursday night after work, first time in forever. When Kevin calls at Friday lunchtime offering the usual weekend – London adventures: drinking, dressing, and drugs – I tell him I can't make it out. He makes a stink about it and I play along, telling him Katie just needs a weekend off, but it's more than that. She might be a big part of my life but I'm still in charge. After telling Kevin I'm out of action, I go upstairs to put her away. I've still got the suitcase I used to keep her in under my bed when I lived at home, and I pack her up: dresses out of the closet, underwear out of the drawer, make-up in its bag, even the wig and brushes from the stand. I put it all neatly into the case, remembering where everything goes to fit without creasing, and slide it back under my bed.

The afternoon is getting on and I take a shower. Under the warm water, eyes shut, the same question that's been going around my head all week is still bouncing: is Stephen going to come over? I could always text him, but with the police charge hanging over him I probably shouldn't. He's never been the sort to call me, instead he just shows up on a Friday and expects a fuck. Normally I don't mind, wouldn't go along with it if I did, 'cause at least it was predictable. After seeing what he's pulled this week, though, I've got no ideas.

When I'm clean I put pyjama bottoms back on, before taking them off and throwing on a shirt and some jeans. Don't bother with socks but spritz some aftershave. Downstairs I pull a bottle of wine out of the fridge and have a look around Netflix for something. After half an hour I just go back to having ITV be the background of my night; it's much easier when the decisions on what to watch are just made for you.

Each time I hear a car drive down my street I listen out for it stopping outside. By the time a crap, late-night film starring Matthew Broderick's stupid face tries to start I've had enough. I flick the box off and turn the kettle on to make myself a brew. As I'm clattering through the cupboards looking for the new box of teabags the doorbell goes. I've been waiting all night for it, and now that it has I freeze up. Do I open it? Two more minutes and I'd have been upstairs, could have pretended to be sound asleep. Perhaps I'm being stupid. It might just be Kevin coming around to check on me. Or the police, about last week. Or—

'Ka— Gar—, please,' shouts Stephen through the letter box. Of course it's him. 'Please,' he says again, 'just open the door up.'

He rings the doorbell again and takes to knocking too. I tiptoe up to the door.

'Please, I just want to talk,' he says, this time by shouting at the door. I could leave him out there, but it'll just end in trouble. He'll annoy a neighbour, and most of them aren't the sorts to call the police to sort this kind of thing out.

'You shouldn't be here,' I say, quiet but forceful, 'police won't be happy if we're talking.'

'You're there? You've . . . please. I got no one else.'

'Go home, Stephen.'

'She found out,' he says, followed by a big sigh. 'She found out, told me to get out or she'd tell everyone.'

'But you shouldn't have come here,' I say.

'Nobody else knows. Can't talk to my mates about it. Can't talk to anyone. Only you.'

I shouldn't open the door, but I know what it's like to be trapped like he is. I slip the chain off, slowly turning the lock to be as quiet as I can, half expecting Stephen to barge onto the door and leap through. That he'd knock me back over, like he had the week before when he'd smacked seven shades out of Samuel. None of that happens, though, and I open the door wide to see Stephen stood on the mat, damp from drizzle. He looks rounder, softer, with red eyes. His white shirt is nearly see through, and his grey trousers are stained with rain. I don't say anything to invite him in, just nod, and he gingerly steps over the threshold into the hallway of the little terrace flat I rent. Normally I leave the door unlocked and he charges straight upstairs for me, don't think he's ever been downstairs. He stands in my tiny hallway, taking up all the space.

'I'm making a cuppa if you want one. How about a towel?' I say.

'Yeah, if it's no trouble. Sorry,' he stutters out.

I pop upstairs and grab a clean towel, and when I'm back down he's still stood in the hallway, blocking it.

'Here,' I say, handing it to him, 'and go sit down, will you?'

He trudges off towards the living room muttering more sorries, and I put the kettle back on. It's still warm and boils quickly.

'How d'you take it?' I ask him, popping my head into the living room. He doesn't look up, and stays sat like a boxer slumped between rounds, towel over his head.

'Tea,' I say to him again, 'how d'you take it?'

'However,' he says from beneath.

I make him a standard milk and two, and sit down next to him on the small sofa.

Space is tight and as he shuffles over slightly our thighs rub together. He leans over me a bit to pick his mug up, blowing on it from under his towel, and putting it back down again. Does it a few times while we sit there in silence.

'What happened?' I ask. He exhales and fidgets, rubbing his palms on his trouser legs.

'Police came around last night, about what happened,' he says. 'Nothing's coming of it, just a caution, but they've got to give it to me. But the wife's there, isn't she? Answers the door. She hears me get it. When they're gone she asks where I really was, what I was up to, not out with my mates obviously.'

'What did you tell her?'

'Tried to say it was nothing, that we got in a pub ruck.

But she heard them say that it was over a girl called Katie. I was stuck. Had no choice then. So I told her. That I wasn't out with my mates. About us. I had to tell her, and when I did she threw me out. Called me a fucking cheater.'

Have to bite my tongue, literal. She's right, he is all those things, and a lot worse. Bit of me wants to ask why he's telling me this like he's the victim, but life doesn't work like that. He's having to confront something, maybe for the first time, and I'm not pushing back against it. Instead I put my hand on his back and knead gently at his neck.

'She called me sick. Fucked up. Made her life a joke. Asked me why I married her, had a kid with her, if I was just going to do this.'

It's all true, but who knows what he'll do if I remind him of that.

'She said she'll tell everyone down at the garage at work, if she does I can't go back. Not the way they talk about people who are, well, like . . . She'll tell everyone. With fucking glee she'll tear it all down.'

He goes on like that, asks me questions about what he should do now, but I don't give him anything; the answers I found for myself aren't going to slot in neat for him, and now's not the time for it anyway. I keep rubbing at his back, reassuring, until he calms down.

'You got somewhere to stay tonight?' I ask him and he shakes his head.

'Hotel, I guess.'

'It's late. Stupid money for a few hours' kip. I'll make the sofa up for you, if you want. Just for tonight.'

I grab a spare blanket from the airing cupboard and take

a pillow off of my bed. While I pour out our cold, undrunk tea he makes up a bed on the sofa. I can tell just by looking that his feet'll stick way over the edge, but I can't turf him out into the night.

'Feel free to turn the telly on if you can't sleep or something. Bathroom's upstairs, turn right,' I say. He doesn't offer a goodnight and neither do I.

I leave him to it and go to bed, changing back into pyjama bottoms before flopping into the sheets. I can't sleep, kidding myself thinking I could. I remember when I had to tell my family. Guy at college caught me online, threatened to tell my parents. I just did it instead. Mum and my brother stuck by me. Dad didn't, but he didn't do anything rash then. Did when he came home and saw me as Katie. He didn't tell Mum and my brother why I was moving out with a black eye that night.

I toss and turn, try browsing my phone a bit, then lay in the dark. I put some music on my little Bluetooth speaker, turn it off, then back on again low. He's down there, and when I hear steps edging their way up the stairs I almost stop breathing to hear him clearly. I track Stephen, hear him turn right into the bathroom. When he's done I hear him close the bathroom door gently. Doesn't go back downstairs, though, so I know he's just stood out there. I pick my phone up and skip the song that's playing to the next one. During the intro I hear him shuffle towards my door. Makes my heart go in my chest like it's my first time.

The door opens a crack and he slips in. I move, slightly, just my legs, trying to let him know I'm aware of things. That it's okay he's there, if you can do that by moving your calves a bit. He sits on the side of the bed, and puts a hand on my hip. I move slightly, raising it and lying more on my side, before settling back down. He lifts up the duvet and lays down next to me, first time we've laid down under the covers together, and I lift my head up to let him put his arm under my neck. He puts his other arm over me, and I grind myself against him slightly. From the way our skin touches, I can tell he's just in his boxers.

We lie there, silent, me pretending I'm mostly asleep and him letting me, despite my heart pounding him out a message to do something. He moves the top of his head right against the back of mine, and I can feel his breath on my neck. We stay like that until he kisses my neck, barely a kiss, more like dragging his dry lips across it, but I grind myself into him again anyway. I can feel him getting hard, and I'm already there. He runs his hand along my chest as his kisses get braver, and eventually it goes lower. He runs his hand over me, brushing his fingers against me lighter than I knew he could, and I let out a heavy breath to encourage him. He slips his hand inside my bottoms, and holds me tighter with the arm under my neck as he gently wraps his hand around my cock and begins to stroke. I thrust into his rhythm too, and can feel him fully hard from behind as he grinds himself against me. I try to move a hand to him to return the favour, but he reaches around with the arm underneath me and holds my arms, still kissing my neck and stroking me, the pace getting quicker. I start to freeze up, he's got me, but Stephen whispers into my ear.

'Shh, just enjoy it.'

I relax as he starts planting little bites along my neck

too, and I'm panting as I feel myself ready to come. I lay on my back a little more and bite down on his forearm as I do climax, leg twitching as he keeps up the pace through my orgasm, slowing down as my cock gets too sensitive, until he lets go. It's the first time he's just been selfless like that, just wanting to pleasure me, and I want him, all of him. I roll over on top of his body, front to front. The orgasm he'd given me is left all over my chest, and he doesn't seem to care that it rubs between us. I look him in the eye and move in. He closes his eyes and moves in too, and we have our first kiss.

At first our lips just touch, almost resting against one another, before they start to explore. My lips pull his apart, tugging gently on his bottom one, before his do the same to mine. Moving quick he wraps one of his arms around my waist and brings the other up to my head, running his fingers through my hair. He squeezes me tight and pulls as best he can at my short hair, and drags me over, whipping me underneath him, pushing me down into the mattress. I'm trapped and I'm jumping up, out of the bed, scrambling to break his grip and trying to stand up but my legs are caught in the duvet. He tries to hang on, keep me pinned down, so I push hard against his chest to slide out onto the floor, sat on my backside. I'm up real quick, though, pressing my back up the wall, panting while he looks pissed.

'The fuck are you playing at?' he asks, and I clock that I'm going to have to go past him to get to the door.

'You grabbed – I'm sorry – last week – I thought that you were – I—' comes stuttering out my mouth. He pushes his jaw forward, face hard.

'I don't mean to be like this,' he says, and I don't know

if the nasty in his voice is directed at me or himself. I stay shut up and do my best just to hold his gaze.

'You know what it's like to be – to be . . .' he says, trailing off.

'To be what?' I ask, calmly and clearly. I want to hear him say it.

'Where I grew up, when I grew up, you couldn't be, you know? Weren't allowed. So I do what I can.'

We stand off in silence. I feel naked and put my arm across my chest, hiding the still-yellow blotch on my ribs from where he'd hit me the week before.

'I don't know what you want from me here,' I say to him.

'Come back to bed.'

'So we're doing this,' I say, real quiet, 'spending the night?'

He shrugs but doesn't move, doesn't look like moving on either.

'This means something, you know. No one stays the night.'

'I don't see people more than once,' he says, answering something I didn't ask.

'You see Katie, not me,' I whisper, 'and you don't treat her great.'

I drop my arm and watch his eyes go to the yellow-purple stain on my ribs. I do my best to stand with my arms down by my sides, exposed, fighting off the primal urge to ball up to stop a predator clawing open my gut.

'You tried to pay me,' I say, 'pay me to not find out who you really are. I watched you and Samuel go at it. Now you're asking to stay over.'

'Come back to bed,' he says again, still firm but working at the duvet, straightening it out and pulling it back into place from where I ran. He lifts my side, and I edge forward. Every sinew is tight like piano wire when I sit. I have to consciously move my legs up to slide under the cover, and lay down where I was earlier, my back to him. He reaches over me with his arm and I stop breathing, but all he does is throw some cover back over me. I'm rigid when he lifts my head up slightly to slide an arm underneath it.

We lay there for a while in silence. I reach up and start brushing against his forearm.

His muscles tighten too. But there we lay, him holding me and me stroking him, until our bodies soften.

'Tomorrow,' he says into my ear, 'we could try going for breakfast. If you want, that is.'

'Yeah.'

I let myself relax into him, and he begins to hold me tighter. As our bodies begin to soften against each other, I feel him get hard again.

When I wake up I roll over into the space in the bed that Stephen should have been in.

I stretch my body before curling back up. I lie, waiting, seeing if any more sleep is around the corner, but can't help but listen out for any signs of life. There's nothing obvious, no shower or a cistern making a racket after a flush. It's only a little place and you'd be able to hear somebody if they were downstairs, but there's nothing. He must be down there if he's not here, and I should wait for him to come back to bed, but get up anyway. He's probably making coffee for us, might be trying to surprise me. I put on a T-shirt and pyjama bottoms and sneak to my bedroom door, feeling like a prize idiot for creeping around my own house.

The bathroom door's open, and there's no Stephen in there. I bang downstairs, hoping that my noise will provoke a good morning from him. The living room has only got the remains of the bed which Stephen half attempted to make, and the kitchen is clear apart from last night's mugs. He's gone, then.

I stare at the two mugs in the sink. Hot water on and some washing up liquid squirted onto the sad sponge to clean the dark rim out of the mug I used. I put it on the draining board and pick up Stephen's. I rinse it and throw the fucker into the metal sink. It smashes into a dozen pieces, enamel flying and pinging off the window in front of me.

'Fuck him,' I say out loud, quiet at first as I grind my bottom teeth against the back of my top ones, before getting louder, 'fuck him, fuck him, fuck him!'

I think there's chips of mug on the floor but I don't give a shit. I walk through them and sit down on the sofa. The cover is still there, and I lay down in the bed which Stephen should have slept in, pull my spare duvet over my head.

I should have known. Of course I should. I think about going upstairs and getting my phone to call him, perhaps he just popped to the shop to get the paper, but I've lied to myself enough, and I'm not even that fucking stupid anyway. Of course he isn't here. He sleeps with Katie, not me. He didn't tell his missus that he was out seeing me, he told her he was out fucking Katie. I'm not Katie, I'm me. She's a part of me, yeah, sure, but she's still just a bit of me and I'm me. And I gave Stephen me, the best I could. But it's my fault, I showed him who I really am and he never sees people more than once.

Acknowledgements

I wrote the first draft of the first story in *The Quarry* in 2013 and have an impossibility of people to thank for things between then and now, plus before and beyond. But here goes . . .

I was blessed to have amazing teachers and fellow students at both Emerson College and Kingston University. The workshops at both forged me as a writer, and that is a testament to the skill and insight of my classmates and tutors. Special thanks to Dr David Rodgers for the readings which were at the heart of my MFA years, Pamela Painter for using her office hours to beat bad habits out of me, and A.J. Hartley for his advice.

To my friends, whether I met you twenty years ago at school, or at a dingy Allston house party in my twenties, I can't imagine life without you. We've made memories in the good times, and you've been there to drown sorrows when things have gone wrong. You've given me places to live when I've had nothing, and gone around the world with me when I've had. I can't wait to celebrate this with you.

Sharmaine, I can only call myself an author today

because of the chance you took on me. I owe you and your team everything, and I will not let you down.

I don't know what to say about my family other than they have supported me in tangible ways which have shown a faith I haven't always had in myself, and I will do everything I can to repay you.

To everyone who has ever read my work, taken the time to give feedback, or just loved me, thank you. Truly, thank you.

Bringing a book from manuscript to what you are reading is a team effort.

Dialogue Books would like to thank everyone at Little, Brown who helped to publish *The Quarry* in the UK.

Editorial
Sharmaine Lovegrove
Thalia Proctor
Sophia Schoepfer

Contracts
Anniina Vuori

Sales
Andrew Cattanach
Ben Goddard
Hannah Methuen
Caitriona Row

Design
Bekki Guyatt
Jo Taylor

Production
Narges Nojoumi
Nick Ross

Publicity
Millie Seaward

Marketing
Emily Moran

Copy Editor
Jon Appleton

Proof Reader
Oliver Cotton